a Bride for Adam

Book #2
Sons of Nora White

CYNDI RAYE

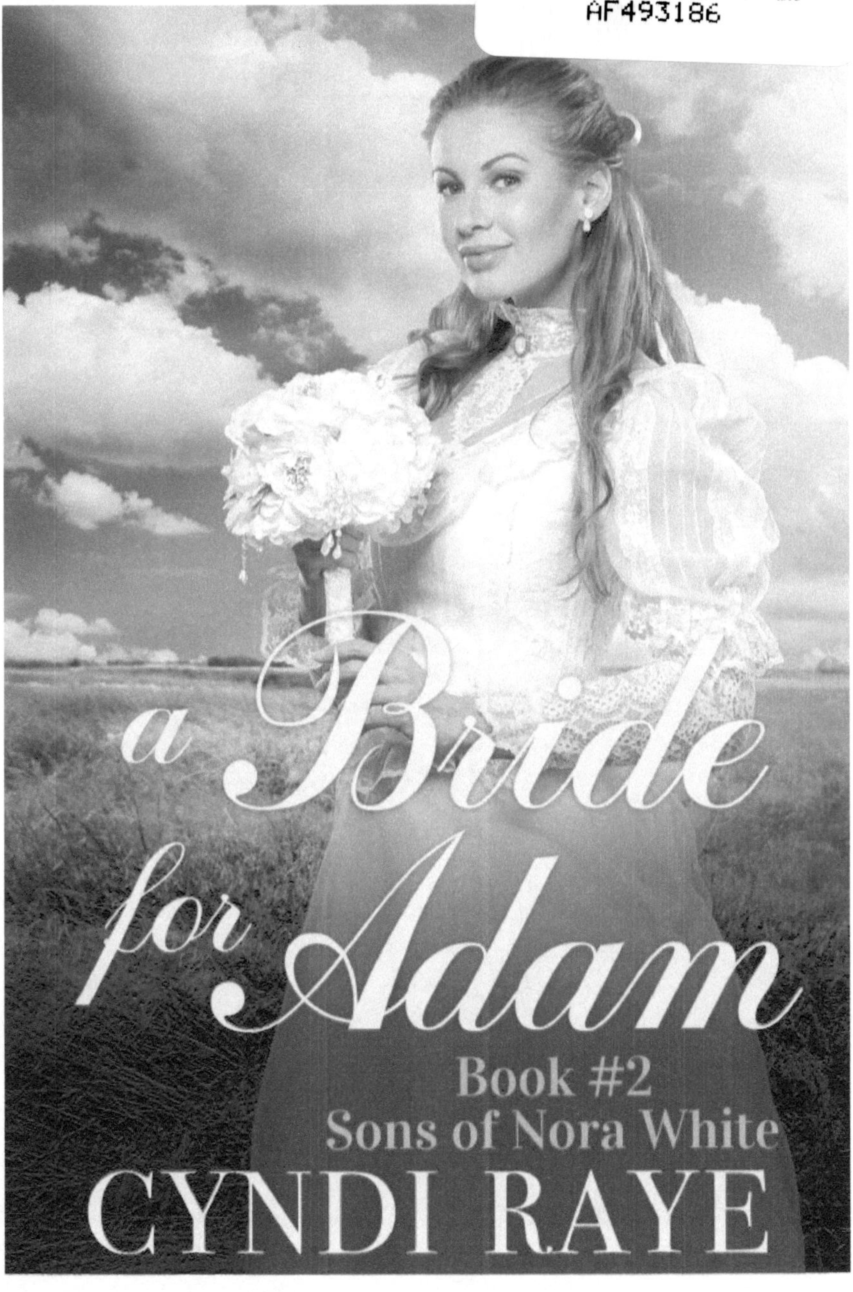

A Bride for Adam

by

Cyndi Raye

Sons Of Nora White

Book #2

<><><>

Cover art by Madison of Silverheart Publishing

1. http://www.CyndiRaye.com

Dedication

Thank you to one of my awesome readers
Barbara Szabo-Orris
for coming up with the name of the small town of Cooper's Ridge.

Chapter 1

"By the power vested in me by the State of Texas, I, Judge Ronald Hanover, now declare Mr. Thomas Cromwell, and wife, Melody Cromwell, standing before me under oath, divorced, by Texas State law." The Judge glared at her, showing his disdain. His brows, thick and bushy, covered the space above his steel framed glasses like a strait line across his brow. "According to the Married Woman's Property Act of 1848 you would be entitled to property if you had any. Since there is none listed here, you are not entitled to any such property in this case."

She stood tall and straight, her shoulders back. Melody was no longer ashamed, although they expected her to be. She was fighting for her life and her son. She didn't dare look around the courtroom because she knew what was there. More disdain and hurtful looks and stares. A woman didn't ask for a divorce in today's society.

"Judge Hanover, sir?"

His frown didn't make her twitch. She vowed to be brave and strong for her sons sake as well as her own.

"What is it?"

"With the courts permission, I would like to ask for sole custody of my son, Tommy." The room stilled. Gloved hands of ladies present in the courtroom flew to their mouths to cover the gasps that represented the negativity in the room. Melody wanted to curl up and hide but held her head high instead. She would not go any lower than she already felt.

Melody didn't turn her head, she stared directly in front of her where Judge Hanover sat on his seat at the helm of the courtroom. Her husband stood to the right with his lawyers. She felt his eyes on her and tried not to wince.

She would not look at him.

She would not show an ounce of fear. Everything was riding on her ability to be a strong, independent woman.

"Let me ask you one question, Mrs. Cromwell, excuse me, Miss Rivers. Now that I officially granted your divorce, we no longer affiliate you with the name Cromwell, a highly respected name in this city."

Melody didn't take the bait. Even the Judge wanted her to fall apart. She would not. "Sir, I will answer any question concerning custody of my son, Tommy."

He nodded, the frown still apparently permanently attached to his face. "How do you plan to support this child, Miss Rivers?"

"I plan to continue to work at my job at Miss Jones Boarding House."

He slowly nodded, raised an eyebrow then turned to speak to Thomas. "Mr. Cromwell, you are a fine, upstanding citizen of Dallas. Are you willing to give custody of your child solely to Miss Rivers?" A few laughs and snickers were heard in some of the pews behind Melody. No man would ever give up custody of their own children. It was unheard of.

Melody didn't realize she had been holding her breath. Tommy was in the Judge's chambers with one of the employees while the trial went on. At least he wasn't privy to all the stares and harsh words and whispers. She clutched her hands together at first, lowering them when she realized how it made her look. She didn't want anyone to see how they shook.

When she realized Thomas was directing his words towards her, she moved her head at a slight angle to peer at him. Her eyes widened in shock at his next words. "Your Honor, I didn't want to bring this up, because it hurts me to paint such a horrid picture of this woman who had me fooled for the last five years."

Melody gasped. How dare he? He was the one who cheated on her and now he was calling her horrid? She was ready to speak up when the next words came tumbling from Thomas's mouth. "I have reason to believe the child is not mine. Therefore, I am not entitled to custody of the child or honored to pay for anything further for *her* son."

He had just told the world his son was not fathered by him!

He had just called her a whore!

In front of the whole courtroom and the Honourable Judge. Melody slumped to her seat. "How can you deny your son?" she whispered, unable to retaliate. She was shocked he had said such a horrible thing.

The Judge stared at Thomas. "Go on, answer, sir, how can you deny the boy? What evidence do you have to say he is not yours?"

Immediately, Thomas's lawyer hurried to the bench, handing over several documents.

He spoke for Thomas. "We believe when the child was conceived, Mr. Cromwell was not present. His work mostly took him out of town. According to a time line we put together, my client was out of town on work during the conception period."

The onlookers gasped.

It was a lie. Melody was speechless for the moment.

These lies were getting worse by the minute. Melody hung her head, not wanting to see anyone's look of scorn. She didn't deserve this, her son didn't deserve to have these lies thrust into the public eye. Thomas was the father, and yet he just threw his son to the side like a piece of garbage.

Anger welled up inside of her, no longer ashamed to face those in the courtroom. If he was determined to deny his son to the world, that only meant one thing. She would receive full custody.

To be called a whore in the public eye was worth it if she got to keep her son. She stood, gripping the wooden rails in front of her. Her lawyer, Donald Cravet, hadn't spoke up during any of this. She actually looked at him in surprise because she barely realized he was even beside her. He hadn't defended her or questioned anything. She had known all along he wasn't much help from the beginning. He took her money and left her here to face the music, alone.

She scowled at him. "You don't have to stand here any more, Mr. Cravet. I haven't had your help since I walked into the courtroom."

Donald Cravet lowered his eyes. He knew he was not going to defend her. It was a man's world and now that she had been called a whore, he was reluctant to even try. Disgust shown in her eyes as she turned away from her lawyer.

The Judge took the hammer and pommelled the desk. "Quiet!" He turned to Melody. "Are these accusations true? Is it a fact Mr. Cromwell is not the father of your son?"

She didn't know what to tell him. To deny he was the father was making her look like a terrible, conniving scam artist. To admit he was the father would make this trial go on longer. For the sake of propriety she wanted the world to know she wasn't a whore. She hadn't been with any man except her husband after they married.

And yet, it was ultimately the purpose of her being here that made her decision. She wanted her son at any cost. Thomas didn't deserve his son, not when he would deny him in front of all these people.

She took a deep breath. *Please God, help me to say the right thing. Help me, Lord, my son doesn't deserve this lying, cheating, no-gooder as a father.* "Judge Hanover, sir, I know my son belongs to me. I am his true parent and would never deny him in front of anyone." She looked at Thomas, the man she had thought she loved, who didn't have the courage to look her in the eye. He stared straight ahead. "I would like it put on the record that I will not deny anything as long as I have full custody of my son."

The Judge frowned even more. He stared at her for the longest time. She refused to cower. Those days were over. If it was known all over Dallas she was a whore then so be it, as long as she walked out of this courtroom with her son's hand in hers.

The Judge shuffled some papers, picked up a pen and began to write. When he looked out in the courtroom, the restless onlookers became still as they waited for the verdict. "By the authority invested in me by the State of Dallas, Texas, I grant the newly named Miss Melody Rivers, full custody of Thomas Michael Cromwell and grant a name change be accepted by the court from Thomas Michael Cromwell to Thomas Michael Rivers." His hammer hit the wood with a ferocity like nothing else. Anger ensued through the Judge's body as he stood up. "Court Adjourned."

Melody dropped her shaking hands to her sides. Even the Judge was angry that she got custody of her son but there was nothing else he could legally do. When Thomas claimed he wasn't the father and did not want the child, the Judge had no other choice. Let them all think what they wanted about her. She no longer cared.

She didn't wait to see the reaction of the people in the courtroom but followed an officer down the hall to pick up her son.

Her son. One hundred percent hers! No one could ever take him away or keep them apart. Being called a whore was worth having her son by her side. It wasn't really a sacrifice at all. Some women would sacrifice more. She was lucky. Darn lucky and she'd never forget the graciousness of this moment.

Melody was a women with full custody of her son. This didn't happen often in courts of law. Which made it more important for her to get him away from this court room as quickly as possible. She didn't want to chance them changing their mind. Not now.

It was a shame his father denied him in front of God and the world but she didn't care any more. Somehow, she would explain things to Tommy so he'd understand the situation. Right now, he needed to be loved, feel loved and kept safe. She wanted to wrap her arms around him and take him far from this horrible place.

In the Judge's chambers, Tommy sat at the big desk, a wooden hammer in his hand. When she called out his name, her five year old son looked up and gave her a smile that was worth waiting for. She held out her hands. "Let's go home."

The boy pushed himself off the big chair and gave the officer a quick hug around his legs. "Good-bye Tommy," the policeman said, waving at the little fellow as he ran into his mother's arms.

Melody held him there, silently thanking God for her son. "Let's get out of here. How about some delicious pastries from the corner shop?"

Tommy jumped up and down, still clinging onto her hand. "Oh, please! I love chocolate filling!"

"Then chocolate, it is!"

<> <>

Melody and Tommy finished their pastry and walked towards the hotel where they had been staying ever since they arrived awhile back. When she had first arrived in Dallas, Thomas didn't welcome her with open arms as she thought he would. Instead, he had put her and Tommy in an adjoining suite, promising to see them daily, except he never kept one promise. He claimed he needed his hotel suite for work and didn't want to be disturbed. Thomas even went as far as locking the adjoining door and demanding she never try to enter into his suite that way.

Being in Dallas was lonelier than she had imagined. Melody almost dreaded the little time they had together. She yearned to be in the arms of her husband but he kept her at a distance as if he didn't even know her. When she complained he demanded she stop harassing him since he was paying for her suite at the nice hotel through *his* hard work.

Melody knew she had to do something to keep her mind occupied. When she saw the sign for help wanted at the local boarding house, she jumped at the chance to make a few dollars on her own. The owner even allowed Tommy to stay with her while she worked. Her husband didn't even know she had a job and so she tucked her weekly pay away. It wasn't much but it didn't hurt to have her own savings since he never spent any money on them. Since he never asked about her day or where she went, she wasn't inclined to tell.

If she had to do it all over again, Melody would never have come to Dallas. She almost wished she had stayed in her little house in Cooper's Ridge, far away from her husband, waiting for him to come home every few weeks. Yet, that kind of life was no way to live either. Looking back, she had done the right thing no matter the pain it had caused. At least now she was living the truth.

Before all this happened, she had become determined to win him over, to find out why he was treating her so differently. There had to be a way to bring them closer, or so she had thought. She had asked one of the ladies from church to watch Tommy one night and went about preparing a lovely evening for the two of them.

Melody had called room service to bring dinner at eight. She was going to surprise Thomas with a delicious meal first and then they would talk. She wasn't about to let him refuse this time. He had always said they can't talk in front of the boy. Well, he was away for the evening and it was time for them to have some time together.

At six o'clock Melody heard noises next door. She had been waiting patiently and quietly to make sure she didn't miss when he got in. Muffled sounds came from his side of the hotel suite. Was someone with him? Oh dear! She knew he brought clients home and hoped they would leave soon so she could continue with her plans.

Two hours later, the dinner had been brought to her suite. Melody held her ear against the wall, wondering if his client had left yet.

What she heard next made her hair stand on end. A woman's laughter pierced her heart and soul. She sounded as if she were right on the other side of the wall, so close that Melody almost jumped back.

Melody was naive but she was pretty certain the woman's soft laughter was not a client of his. Everything came together all at once, imploding her brain with mass upon mass of signs she had not recognized at first. The late nights at work. His refusal to eat dinner with her and Tommy, claiming he was working. No marital relations.

The dirty, rotten low down no-gooder had been seeing another woman all along! Or maybe more than one! All she knew at that particular moment was the fact she was not going to allow him to get away with this for another second!

Melody flew out of her suite and began knocking on his door. She didn't say a word. Her knocking got louder when she realized it was being ignored.

"One moment!" Thomas's voice was strained but he finally must have realized someone was there. When the door was flung open, she had stood there, hands on her hips.

A drunken Thomas held a whiskey filled glass casually in his hand while the other was still resting on the door knob. His face went from a smile to a shocked look when he realized who stood outside his door. "Melody! What are you doing here at my door? I'm drowning in work!" He paused for a moment, looked to the right of him where the other woman was most likely standing.

"Who are you with?" Melody demanded. Her heart was breaking in two. It was crushed. Except now she had realized he had been cavorting with a woman since she had arrived. Melody now realized why he hadn't wanted her here in Dallas.

He had tried to shut the door. Melody pushed against the wood, causing Thomas in his drunken state to stumble. He kept his glass steady and held it up as if it were more important to make sure no liquor splashed out. "I warned you not to disturb me, Melody!"

She had flung terrible words in his face. "You are a lying, cheating, rotten, womaniser. A no-gooder who doesn't have an ounce of gentleman in you!"

Melody had wanted to strike the woman who stood there, her back against the wall that separated Thomas from his family. She was a beautiful blonde, dressed impeccably, her hair in place and wearing expensive clothing. She seemed mildly surprised then stared at Melody while taking a sip from the elegant wine glass. Her emotions were hiding behind a perfect face.

"Melody, go back to your suite. I'll join you in a moment so we can talk."

Melody's tears fell. She swiped at them, more angry at herself for failing to hold them in check. "We are finished. You and I. There will be no talk or conversation to say you are sorry. I want a divorce."

Thomas laughed. She was stunned he had the audacity to laugh in her face. "You will never be granted a divorce. Go back to the suite Melody. We will deal with this later."

She had turned on her heels and left his suite, slamming the door with such fury it popped back open. That's when she heard their laughter.

Melody had stood outside the room, listening to their conversation, horrified.

Her husband had apologized to the woman for the insult to her sensibilities. Melody had been ready to march back inside but deemed it futile. Then she heard him say such awful things she actually placed both hands over her ears. Even though her feet were able to move, she stood frozen to the floor, enduring the conversation.

"She won't tell anyone, Mary. Melody has no one, her parents are living far off in Montana or one of those primitive wilderness places. She'll behave like a proper wife should."

Melody was in shock that he'd say such a thing. He went on after the woman had mumbled something Melody wasn't able to understand.

"I married her because the law firm requires a family man in order to move up to become a partner. I had no intention of having her here in Dallas. Everything was fine until she moved here. Now, I'm stuck with a wife next door and a kid. I don't even like kids."

You are far from stuck, Thomas! I will make sure you never touch me or see our son again!

His words prompted Melody to seek a lawyer with the determination of a woman on a mission. With some of the money she had saved, she had hired Mr. Cravet to petition the courts for a divorce. The lawyer had been surprised and warned her it was not likely she'd be granted one but Melody had insisted. She had been lucky the lawyer was able to get them on the docket in less than a few weeks. Everything had moved so fast.

While waiting for the trial, and feeling utterly trapped inside the suite for a week, she had been determined to make the four hour trip to the White Ranch after receiving a telegram from Nora White. Nora was throwing a wedding celebration for her oldest son Luke and his new wife. While there, Abigail had found out about the impending divorce case and made Melody promise to come back to the White Ranch when it was over. Melody had promised she would but at the time had little faith her divorce would ever be granted.

Now here she was, divorce granted!

Her heart was heavy. Tommy had been getting used to city life, loving the carriage rides and walking to the park when they had a chance. He even loved tagging along to the boarding house to be treated with home-made cookies and creamy milk.

She stood at the large hotel for a few seconds, Tommy's hand in hers. "Are we going home, Mommy?"

Home right now was a large, intimidating hotel that housed her and Tommy as well as her now former husband. Since she never saw much of him before, she guessed they would try to make a go of it on their own. Tommy didn't even ask after his father. It saddened Melody to know she failed to keep her marriage and give him the kind of family he deserved.

"Yes, Tommy. This is home for now."

"I miss the horses, Mommy." He bounced up and down. "I want to go see PaPa Rusty."

She picked up Tommy, wanting him close to her and ran across the street. "Soon, Tommy. I still have to put in a few hours of work at the boarding house. Would you care to come along with me?" He loved the ranch but she was afraid now that she'd have to do the supporting, her job would keep her in the city. She didn't have time to go to the ranch.

"Oh, yes! I love work!"

Melody smiled as they made their way into the hotel. She needed to change into her work dress and gather up some items for Tommy to keep himself occupied before they made their way to the boarding house. When she walked across the entry way, a sudden quiet chilled her bones. It wasn't a good feeling.

The proprietor, Mr. Williams, stood at the staircase Melody and Tommy always used to get to the second floor. He held up a hand. "Wait, right there, Miss Rivers." How did he know she was divorced and had a name change? He always called her Mrs. Cromwell.

"What seems to be the problem, sir?" Melody was starting to get nervous. "I need to get through to my room."

He coughed then, trying to clear his throat. The man had always treated her kindly. His cheek twitched, as though he was nervous. He avoided looking into her eyes. Something was wrong and she had a feeling it had to do with Thomas.

"I'm sorry, Miss Rivers. As of this moment, you no longer have a suite here that is paid by Mr. Cromwell. He has stopped payment on the room. I'm sorry, unless you can pay the daily rate, we must ask you to leave."

Her voice was hoarse as she whispered, "What is the daily rate?"

Melody almost fell to her knees when the proprietor quoted a figure she would never be able to afford on her pay. "I can't possibly come up with that amount. Will you take five dollars? I can pay you for one more night if you'd accept five dollars?"

Mr. Williams shook his head. "The truth is I can't accept anything from you, ma'am. Not even if you have the exact amount. Mr.

Cromwell is a top-notch customer and we must honor our regulars. He asked if we would oust you from that suite and I'm afraid under these dire circumstances, on behalf of this facility, I must ask you to leave."

Terror and fear strangled her throat. "Where can I go with a small child? You can't possibly throw me out on the street?" How could Thomas let his own wife and son live on the streets of a big city?

"I don't know, ma'am. Perhaps the boarding house where you work will take you in. If that's what you are doing there day after day."

She placed a hand to her hip. "What is that supposed to mean!"

He shrugged. "Rumor has it -"

Melody pinched her side to remind herself to stay calm. It wasn't worth fighting with a man who was given orders. She was so calm headed but what she wanted to do was scream and kick her feet at anyone who got in her way. Except she was a lady. There was no way she would lose her temper.

"Very well. Where are my belongings?"

The proprietor pointed to a large cart on the sidelines of the St. George hotel's lobby. Everything she owned was there. Clothes, dishes, small furniture and more trinkets she had brought with her just a short while ago. Her whole life was changing right in front of her eyes.

Surely, it couldn't get any worse?

Chapter 2

"Would it be too much to ask if I may leave my belongings here until I've secured a place for the evening?"

Mr. Williams nodded. "I don't see how that will hurt any. I'm sorry again, ma'am, I'm under strict instructions here. I'll keep your belongings right where they are for twenty-four hours. Will that give you adequate time?"

Melody nodded.

"What's wrong, Mommy? Why can't we go home? There's daddy, that no good, rotten, swindling -"

"Tommy! Do not repeat words you hear."

"You said them first, Mommy."

She swung around to see Thomas and his companion, their arms intertwined, making their way across the lobby. He refused to look her way, even when she stared at him in contempt. How can he throw away five years of their life this way?

Melody bent down. "Tommy, go over to our belongings on the cart over there and wait, please." She made sure the boy did as told and marched across the lobby before Thomas and the woman made it to the stairwell. "Thomas, I wish to speak to you."

He turned slowly, looking over her head, not directly into her eyes. He was a coward. Why she wanted an answer was beyond her. What had she seen in this man for the last five years?

"We are no longer married, Melody. I suggest you be on your way. I am not obligated to keep a suite here for you now that you are no longer my wife if that's what you wanted to know."

She placed fisted hands on her hips. "There is such a thing as courtesy. Why not at least allow me some time to find another place to live? You would allow us to live on the streets of Dallas like paupers? Is that all you think of me? I was there by your side as you went through law school. She certainly wasn't there to encourage you the last year when you wanted to quit."

It gave her some satisfaction when he winced. Yet, he lifted his chin as if he were arrogant royalty. "I didn't ask you to come here, did I? Now you know the truth and can't handle the consequences. You should have stayed away."

Melody wanted to lash out but she refrained. If she hadn't caught him, everything would've been fine. He would've continued to see other women and lead the life of a successful attorney with a family waiting at home in the wings, representing him as a family man.

Her lips quivered slightly but she forced them to stop. This man would not see her fall apart. She'd leave that for later, when she was alone. "You didn't have to throw us out on the street like some homeless urchins. At least give us time to adjust and find another place to live. I've got a small child to keep safe!"

He lifted one shoulder. "I don't see how you didn't see this coming! Once you made this all public, I had to defend my honor. Cromwell is a strong, well-known family name here in Dallas. I can't allow you to taint the name. Now I have to erase all traces of you from this dear city. Go on back to your friends at that stinky ranch you love so much."

He always had hated when she went to visit her grandfather at the White Ranch. She knew they would never see eye to eye. He was throwing her out on the streets like a rag doll to fend for herself. It was a cruel, heartless act of a man with no heart.

She wanted to hurt him back in that moment. "Maybe I plan to stay right here and taunt you the rest of my life. Beware, Thomas, look behind you and around every single turn as I may be there, waiting to taint your name. You disgust me!"

Thomas shook his arm loose from the blonde woman. He loomed closer, bringing his nose almost next to hers. His voice, low and angry so no one else heard, shook her to her core. "I swear Melody, if you try to cause me trouble I will make sure your son will be put in an orphanage."

The threat caused her to step back. "You can't do that!" Did he think she was daft. "You no longer have any say in his life. Or, mine! I've gotten full custody of him from the courts."

Then he laughed, a cruel, heartless sound. It was the first time she saw such a horrid side of him. Granted, he had been gone more than he was home during their five years of marriage. Did she ever really know this man? "You are wrong. As long as you stay here in Dallas and have no roof over the kid's head is cause enough for him to be sent to an orphanage as a vagrant. I can ask the court to send him there out of concern for a child's safety."

"You wouldn't dare! An orphanage means no parents. Do not try anything foolish, Thomas!"

"The powers that be will listen to me, not you. I'm well known in this city!" he threatened again. "Now, get out of this hotel before I turn the attention on the fact you no longer have a home for the boy."

Melody checked the baggage cart to make sure Tommy was still there. He was sitting on a carpetbag, playing with one of his wooden toys. She needed to protect him at all costs, no matter what. She turned and marched up to the woman, the one who broke up their marriage, wanting to at least have a final word before she left this hotel forever. The blonde stood close by watching her with an amused look on her face.

Melody lifted her chin. "You better enjoy him while you can!"

The blonde woman smirked. "But, I do!" She slid her arm through Thomas's as if she owned him.

"For now you do, I'm sure. What will you do when he tires of you like he did me? You'll be standing right here like I am, watching him on the arm of another woman!"

The blonde was no longer smiling.

"Go!" Thomas barked. "You leave now or I'll have you thrown out!"

The proprietor of the hotel hurried up to them. "Is there a problem?" he asked, directing his question to Thomas.

Thomas stared at Melody.

Would he have her thrown out? In front of Tommy?

She wasn't about to wait to find out. "I'm leaving. I'll be back for my things."

"Twenty four hours, that is as long as I can hold your belongings," the proprietor repeated. He did seem apologetic but money talked in this hotel and she didn't have enough.

"Don't you worry. I'll be back as soon as I find another place to stay."

Melody walked with her head high and her heart shattered. She called for Tommy, who jumped from the carpetbag to join up with her. As the two left the hotel lobby, Melody began to realize exactly what she was up against. If she stayed here in Dallas, he would try to have Tommy put away. Without much money, she didn't have too many choices.

At least she had a job.

Yesterday when she had left the boarding house where she cleaned rooms, there were two available for rent. She hoped they were still there. Perhaps Mrs. Hopper would let her stay in one until she figured out what to do and where to go. At least it was a start. Having a room didn't qualify her son as a vagrant. Relief flooded through her. She'd show Thomas once and for all he was not going to get the upper hand.

She remembered the promise she had made to Abigail, Luke's wife from the White Ranch. She had told Abigail when this whole ordeal was over, her and Tommy would go there. Abigail was the only other person that knew about the divorce. She hadn't even told Rusty, her grandfather. There was no use worrying everyone. It was her problem.

She wanted to make it on her own first, to live on her own and be able to provide for her son. Melody didn't want to be a failure, to have to go back and beg for help. At least she had to try to be independent. There had to be jobs available, the city was growing by leaps and bounds every day.

After she established herself here, by starting over, then she'd go visit the ranch and let Abigail know they were doing fine, but first she had to get things in order here. She also wanted to prove to Thomas she didn't need him, that she was fine on her own. Why did she even care what he thought? Or maybe not so much Thomas, but herself.

Melody thought it odd the door to the boarding house was locked when she arrived. She tapped on the door several times until there was a noise from the other side. The door swung open to reveal an older lady with pure white hair stuffed under a bonnet of sorts.

"Is everything alright, Mrs. Hopper? Why is the door locked?"

Mrs. Hopper glared at her. "To keep riff-raff out!" She began to shake her finger at Melody, some of the wrinkles jiggling on her cheeks.

Melody had a bad feeling all of a sudden. She moved Tommy behind her, patting him on the shoulder. "Stay," she warned, not knowing what words the two would exchange. Melody had a feeling Mrs. Hopper's anger had to do with her newly announced divorce she was sure everyone knew about now that the trial was over.

"You are not to set foot inside of my boarding house, young lady. Do I make myself clear? I can't have your type here with my guests! Now go on, be on your way!"

Melody was almost tongue-tied at the older woman's words. "What about my job?" How in the world was she going to support herself and Tommy? Without this job she'd truly be a vagrant.

"I can't have you here among my renters. Your presence will disgrace this business. Now, please, before I call for that nice policeman across the street, you best be on your way."

The door slammed in her face. Melody wanted to slump to the ground and cry. Tears teetered on the rim of her eyes but she wasn't going to fall apart. Not now. Not when Tommy was looking at her with fear in his own little eyes.

"Mommy? Why is Mrs. Hopper being such a meanie?"

"She's having a bad day. Come along, Tommy, let's take a nice walk."

Where in the world would they sleep tonight? She had no home to go back to, even if it had been a hotel suite, it had become their temporary home. How dare Thomas do this to her!

They strolled the streets for some time, visiting shops on Main Street to see if there was a position to be filled. Melody checked the Market Drug Store in hopes they needed a clerk but was treated as if she had a contagious disease. They hadn't even given her a chance to speak before asking her to leave.

Every single place either ignored her or plainly told her there was no room in their store for a divorced woman. She walked along Elm Street, checking with Dr. Thomas, the local dentist who had a help wanted sign in his window but when she got there the place was locked up. A clerk in Rick's Furniture store below the dentist shop said the Dentist had been placed in an insane asylum for odd behavior.

The furniture store didn't have any openings but at least the proprietor wasn't mean like everyone else. She moved from store to shop until every single place of business had refused her. Melody had to cover Tommy's ears at times so he didn't hear the awful names they called her. She hadn't realized how fast gossip spread until she became a victim herself.

After hours spent wandering, she spotted a help wanted sign in a small café across from the St. George Hotel. They had walked full circle without any luck finding work.

"Can we get something to eat? I'm hungry!" Tommy rubbed his belly. His little feet were dragging along, trying to keep up.

"Of course. Let's take a seat here by the window." The two settled in while waiting for someone to take their order. Ten minutes later Melody ordered a bowl of soup and some crackers for Tommy. She didn't choose anything for herself, afraid to spend any more money than necessary. She needed to be careful right now, making sure she had enough for a room for the night.

It was getting later by the hour. Perhaps staying in Dallas wasn't feasible any longer, not the way she was treated. She sighed. Trying to make it on her own was near impossible when everyone turned her away. Wasn't there anyone in this town who didn't know she just got a divorce? How did word travel so quickly?

Regret began to eat at her inside and out. As she pushed strands of loose hair that had fallen from the neat bun she had arranged earlier, Melody longed for the tender words of her best friend. Adam White had always been there for her, from the very first time she had visited the White Ranch during those summers when she was young. Her parents had loved going to the ranch to spend their summer vacation there. She had always looked forward to leaving the city to spend time with her grandpa at the ranch. And Adam and his brothers.

They had done everything together. The times they had gone swimming together in the creek on the ranch, rode their horses across the prairie as if they were going into a battle and she even learned how to rope a calf one summer. Adam had been so much fun. They even sliced their fingers one year, combining their blood to declare to be best friends for life. She smiled as the memories came back. Everyone who lived there knew of their special friendship.

She knew the White Ranch would take her in. Melody had promised Adam's sister-in-law, Abigail, she'd leave Dallas and go to the ranch after her divorce. She just didn't realize it was going to be so soon. It seemed that in Dallas, there was no way for a divorced woman to start over.

The whole city spewed gossip like a rabid dog. All it took was one person who knew she was newly divorced and the news spread like wildfire. Shop after shop had refused to hire her, some even bluntly told her why. Others claimed they filled the position right before she arrived even though she knew it was a lie.

The café was the last place to try to get a job in the immediate area. Now she had other worries as well. It would soon be nightfall and they'd have to find somewhere to sleep. The thought worried her. At least she had her own wagon and horse. If they had to go to the livery and sleep in the wagon, at least they'd be safe there. Her life was full of options, but none that made her feel better. If she were to be found sleeping in her wagon, would the police arrest her for vagrancy? She had no job, no place to stay. Unless the café gave her a job.

When it was time to pay for the soup, Melody asked to speak to the owner.

"That's me," the woman who waited on her announced. "Name's Doris Stauffer."

"I saw the sign in the window and would like to apply for the position."

"Can you wait on tables and do dishes?"

Melody smiled. "I can do whatever it is you need done. I'll work hard."

"What about the little one there. What will you do with him while you work?" The woman began to wipe down the table next to them while they talked.

"If I may bring him along, I'll be sure to keep him occupied while I'm working. At least until I can find someone to care for him." Melody's hopes began to soar once again. Finally, something good was happening. She offered to start first thing in the morning.

"Sure, why not. I'll be right back, my cook needs me." The owner left, hurrying through the door to the kitchen.

Five minutes later, the owner came back to their table. By the look on her face, Melody already knew she lost the job before she ever had it. The look on the owner's face was the same as everyone else. She stood. "Come along, Tommy."

"I'm sorry," she told Melody. "I'll lose business if I hire you. I have to feed my family, too."

Melody left the café, dejected and so down on her luck, she stood on the side walk holding Tommy's little hand. What were they going to do? A tear fell and she brushed it away, trying to compose herself before Tommy realized how upset she was.

When she had stood in that courtroom early this morning knowing she would be called a whore and rejected by anyone who crossed her path, she hadn't cared at the time. The most important person in her life was holding her hand, trusting her to keep him safe. Even though her reputation was now ruined, her son would be with her and not raised by a man who didn't even want to claim him as his own. This was her focus. Her life. She would leave here and by going to the White Ranch, it would keep her from exposing little Tommy to these heartless people.

She had to find a place to stay for tonight. There was no sense in trying to travel in the dark. The White Ranch was four hours from here, not a short jaunt by any means. They'd have to stay in the wagon tonight and head out at the light of day after picking up their belongings at the hotel.

Melody searched for signs that led them to the livery. Since she had come to the city, she had it housed at the livery and that's where it had stayed all this time. When they arrived at the stables, little Tommy was yawning. Melody picked him up and held him while he fell asleep with his head on her shoulder.

A friendly fellow was closing up. He was getting ready to douse out the lamp. "Sir, can you help us?"

"Why, hallo Miss. What can I do for you? My name is Don Welch."

She didn't enjoy telling stories but for the sake of her son she made up a lie. "My husband is terribly drunk and threatened to hurt the boy. I don't want to go back home until he gets sober. May we spend the night here in our wagon, which is over yonder? I can pay you."

Don Welch shook his head. "I swear these men don't know what good they have in their lives and don't appreciate nothing. The darn drunken lot of them. You go right ahead, Miss, I'll leave one of the lanterns by the door on for you. Keep it down so you don't rattle the livestock in here. They like it nice and serene."

Relief spread through her body like a tornado over a Kansas prairie. "Thank you kindly, Mr. Welch. Here, let me pay you."

Don Welch stepped back and put up a large hand. "No, ma'am, it's the least I can do for you. I'm sorry you have to sleep outside your home. You may want to think things through before going back to a drunkard."

Tommy stirred in her arms. "I certainly will, sir. Thank you."

"Your welcome. I'm locking you in now, so you won't be able to leave until I unlock the door at first light. I like to get here a half hour before it gets busy. That should give you and the boy some time to catch up on some sleep and your husband to sober himself up."

Melody climbed in the wagon, which was now empty and placed her son in the corner. In the morning, she'd have to take the wagon and park it in front of the hotel to load up her and Tommy's belongings. She shook off her shawl and placed it over him. His little body curled up in a fetal position. She leaned against the side of the wagon, placing a hand on Tommy's back to let him know she was right there. At first light, Mr. Welch would open up and they'd have to leave.

At least they were safe for tonight. If Thomas knew they were sleeping in this wagon, he'd have the authorities take Tommy away. Even though he didn't care what happened to them his threats were real. His heartless soul would call the police to get them out of his hair for good.

It was an awful, drastic feeling to be abandoned by the man you thought loved you and would be in your life forever.

Melody curled next to Tommy, listening to her belly growl. She hadn't eaten anything today but at least they would have money to get to the White Ranch tomorrow. She'd stock up fresh water for the horse and some food for them to take along.

She had to be realistic, it was her duty as a mother to make sure her son was safe. This was no life for a child, to wander the streets of a city with her to find work. No one wanted her here. Not a divorced woman. She was shunned the moment she allowed the courts to call her a whore. Abigail had known she'd be treated badly, it must've been why she had made Melody promise to return to the ranch.

Melody felt like a failure. As a wife, a mother and provider.

She fell asleep with a heavy heart. Curling an arm around her son, she vowed to make a better life for them, somehow, some way. Even if she wasn't able to see what the future would bring.

All she knew was she had to try.

Chapter 3

Adam sat on the grassy bank staring at the trickling water flowing downstream in the creek. His two brothers, Luke and Samuel, sat close by. Samuel was spread out on his back, watching a butterfly land on a tree limb while Luke sat with elbows on knees, breathing heavy as if he had wrestled more than the rest of them. The three of them always seemed to wind up in a wrestling match at any known time. It had become a habit since childhood.

Adam rubbed his jaw, the dark stubble of a beard beginning on his chin. He hated shaving but did so for Sunday church meetings.

It was one request his Ma always made so Adam obliged. He loved his mother more than anyone or anything. She had raised him and his two brothers after their Pa had died over ten years ago.

"A penny for your thoughts?" Luke, the oldest, asked, grinning.

Adam shrugged, picking up a piece of grass to place between his teeth. "You always say that. I was thinking about Ma and how we've kept this secret from her for the last ten years or so."

Luke nodded. "A secret that will never be spoken aloud. I know sometimes my wife is suspicious there is something going on between the Youngs and our ranch, but I can usually avert her questions. She is so close to Ma, I'm afraid if I told her she would not be able to keep it to herself. I can't afford to upset Ma."

"More like devastate her. Thanks for not telling Abigail, Luke. I guess it's my turn now to bring home a wife. The cabin is almost ready for a bride." Adam stared hard at the landscape beyond the creek. The thought of getting married didn't make him happy, it saddened him because the one he truly wanted belonged to someone else.

Samuel's laughter was meant to tease his brother. "Adam's getting married!"

"Shut up, Samuel. You'll be the next one!"

"I don't want to ever get married. Ma can try all she wants but I'm staying right here enjoying my life on the ranch without a crazy woman to follow me around day and night."

Luke grinned. "You may find it's not so crazy after all. Especially when you have someone to sit on the porch watching the sunset at night, or making sure you're well fed before leaving for work."

Samuel laughed again, a little louder. "You are crazy! I've got that right now! Why, Ma makes the best breakfast in the whole land! And for the porch sitting, you can forget that, I'd rather be sitting on a bale of hay in the barn playing a game of poker with the men."

Adam grinned. "He got you there, Luke."

Luke sighed. "It ain't the same. Adam, you'll find out soon enough. Ma just received a letter the other day about your new bride. Did she give it to you yet."

"Yeah, she did but I haven't read it."

Luke frowned. "Well, what are you waiting for? Read it and get prepared. Your cabin will be done by this weekend at the latest. You better find out when your supposed to get to Wichita Falls to meet her on the train if she's coming the way my bride did."

When his Ma offered him a parcel of land to build a cabin for his new mail-order bride she ordered, Adam knew it was a matter of time before the deal was sealed. He did agree to have a mail order bride, solely for the fact he knew it was time to settle down. Watching Luke these last few months made him realize he wanted more from life than to ranch. He wanted a woman by his side, someone to spend late nights with star gazing or taking long walks hand in hand.

Adam longed for the days when his best friend would spend the summer. Melody. Sweet Melody. She was everything he had wanted in a woman, in a bride. Sadly, she belonged to someone else.

Not being able to ever claim Melody as his bride made Adam realize he may as well settle for a mail order bride that his Ma had picked out. If he wasn't able to be with Melody, he guessed a second choice would have to work. He hated to think that way but Melody was the only woman he had ever wanted as a wife.

She had the sweet laugh of an angel. Placing his arms across his knees, Adam heard in his mind her zealous laugh when they would ride, how her hair was set free and the long auburn waves tumbled down her back. She'd push them up under her hat when they got back to the ranch but she loved riding astride, racing over the meadows and through the valleys, claiming she felt as free as the wind here on the prairie.

He knew his Ma rode like the dickens too, so she really wasn't ever able to reprimand Melody. Even her parents had chosen to let her be free during the summers she spent on the ranch. He flat out missed her. The last five years had been so dull except for the times she came to visit Rusty.

She had showed up one time after she had married that rich city lawyer, her belly so big he had made a point to follow her around in case she tired out. He remembered wishing it was his child. After Tommy was born they came to visit and he held her son in his arms. The boy cooed and Adam wished he had fathered the baby.

Later, after Tommy learned to walk, Melody often showed up because her husband was in the city working and she wanted to teach her son what life was like on a ranch. Adam pretended she came to visit him. Except he had to accept the fact she was a happily married woman. But a man could dream.

Melody lived a half hour away in a small town called Cooper's Ridge. It was a slow growing town but nothing like the city of Dallas.

Melody and Tommy would stay at the ranch now and again since her husband was working on becoming a partner at a law firm in the city and was never home. But then he always showed up at the ranch to fetch her, to whisking her back home to Cooper's Ridge for a weekend jaunt until he headed back to the city, leaving her alone once again.

Adam had to put her out of his head. She was married and happy. Her life now was in the big city of Dallas where she had finally moved to. It was a far cry from ranch life. She had come back once for Luke and Abigail's wedding reception, without her husband. Melody had been too quiet and he wondered if something was wrong. But before he got a chance to talk to her, she was gone. He remembered how his heart dropped to the ground when he found out she left without saying goodbye, something she never failed to do before. It made Adam realize he wasn't an important part of her life any more.

"You still thinking of Melody?" Luke asked, trying to keep his voice low so Samuel didn't hear. It had only been a few weeks since he saw her last. It was eerie how his older brother read his mind at times.

"I can hear you, even though you don't think I can." Samuel sat up, scooting closer to the others.

"I don't want you making a joke of this," Luke told the youngest brother. "Adam cares a lot for Melody."

The three sat along the bank, quiet for some time. Adam was glad Samuel stayed silent and didn't crack any more jokes. Luke was right. He cared way too much for Melody to have Samuel or anyone make a mockery of his feelings.

Even so, it was time to move on. No sense wishing for something he'd never have. She was simply out of reach. "I think it'd be best if I went ahead and got hitched. I'll read the letter later tonight."

Samuel tried to lighten the mood. He was the joker of the three. "Come on, Adam, read it out loud so we can all have a good laugh!"

Adam turned. He pounced on his youngest brother and before long the three were back to wrestling for the next half hour. After all, they still had time until the fences on the lower end had to be checked.

<><>

Adam stared at himself in the small square mirror above the three drawer night stand in his room. He rubbed his jaw, wondering if he would continue to shave each week or let himself grow a beard like some of the farmers did. He grinned. It didn't much matter either way. He guessed once he got hitched, his wife would demand he be clean shaven to go to church, too.

If he were to be honest with himself, Adam didn't really care either way. If he had to marry a mail order bride, then he'd conform to whatever she wanted. He'd try to make her happy, even though she would never get his heart. It already belonged to someone else.

Adam sat on the edge of the bed unable to get her out of his head. He still wondered what Melody was doing now. Was she serving her husband dinner, laughing and teasing like she had done here whenever her and Tommy came to the ranch? Did she look up at him like she did Adam, her beautiful eyes filled with laughter and sunshine?

He shook himself. Enough of this torture! It didn't do him any good to rehash the past. Melody was happy right where she was, in the arms of another man. Adam swiped the back pocket of his pants, pulling the letter out.

Dear Mr. White,

I've just received word from matchmaker extraordinaire Miss Addie of Wichita Falls that you would be honored to choose me as your mail order bride. According to the rules and regulations bestowed upon me, I am told we are to be married immediately upon my arrival in Wichita Falls. I've read the contract and agree to the clause where we have three months to annul the marriage if, and excuse my boldness, we do not consummate the marriage.

My dear husband to be, I can safely say when we become married, I have no intention of any type of annulment on my end. I will be happy to stay married to you for life because my vows I take seriously. I am a lady, I assure you, just very forward and modern. I'm sure once you get to know me, you will ascertain the same thing. It is my understanding you are looking for a bride who will share life on the ranch with you. I will be honored to be that bride.

Yours truly,

Your future Mrs. White

Adam grinned. She sure was outspoken, although she never mentioned her name. Still, he rolled his eyes, folded the letter up and placed it on the top of the night stand. Adam stretched on his back, placing both hands behind his head. She wasn't Melody, would never be like the woman who stole his heart.

But it was time he let go. He picked up the letter, taking out the photo and staring at it, but all he saw was Melody's sweet face. He closed his eyes and still her beautiful face would not go away. If he could get through one night without seeing her in his mind, maybe he would be able to make a future with this mail order bride. Was it fair to keeping thinking of Melody when he should be dreaming of a future with his mail order bride? He needed to purge another man's wife from his mind completely.

It was hours until Adam's eyelids became heavy. He stared out the lone window for the longest time, watching a dark sky as it filtered the clusters of stars, making the night appear brighter than usual as a full moon peeked from behind the barn. Her face danced in his dreams that night, even though he swore he'd try to forget her.

Was he kidding himself? It felt as if he had loved her since forever.

<> <>

Mr. Welch called from inside the barn, disturbing her sleep. "Miss, it's morning, time to be on your way."

Tommy groaned next to her, causing Melody to open her eyes. "I'm so sorry," she cried out, sitting up so quickly it made her feel dizzy. She focused her eyes on Tommy, who still lay curled up, his little fists rubbing the sleep from his eyes.

"Mommy?"

'I'm here, son. Time to get up."

He hopped onto her lap for his usual morning hug. It didn't seem to matter where he had spent the night as long as he woke up with his mother close by. His sleepy smile had Melody returning it with one of her own, even if there wasn't much to smile about. "We must get moving, son."

"Where are we going? I'm hungry?"

"We'll eat after we load up our belongings." She didn't want to go back to the café where he had eaten the night before, not knowing how they would be treated. Some folks in this city were plain mean to a divorced woman. She wasn't going to subject Tommy any longer.

"Good morning, Mr. Welch."

"Morning, ma'am. You'd best get on home now, before there's trouble."

Melody figured Mr. Welch worried her husband was going to come looking for her and cause trouble. That was hardly likely. Trouble, maybe, but he wouldn't be looking for her or Tommy. "No need to worry, we'll hitch up our horse and be on our way."

Ten minutes later, Melody pulled the brim of her hat lower to wield the sunlight from her eyes. "Let's stop at the mercantile first and I'll let you choose something from there for breakfast, Tommy."

He pumped his little body up and down on the seat, clapping his hands. "Thanks, Mommy! I get to choose. I'm so happy!"

His happiness was contagious. In all reality, her life here was over but it was a new day, there were new challenges on the horizon. All she wanted to do was to get the two of them out of Dallas, far away from Thomas and mean people who cared more about their stature than people.

She held her head up high, taking Tommy by the hand as the two walked through the door at Fred Willows Mercantile. They wouldn't need much for the four hour trip to the White Ranch but she wanted to make sure Tommy ate something for breakfast. She was able to wait until she had some of Nora White's good home cooking. Besides, it would be less expensive if she didn't spend the money on herself.

"Good morning, ma'am and little sir. What brings you here so early this morning?"

Melody gave him a smile, relieved he didn't know who she was. "We are on our way to my grandfathers and my son would like something for breakfast to hold him over until then. I'm afraid we don't have time to stop at the café."

Fred Willow put up his one finger, tilting his head and pushing up his spectacles as if he had to think. Melody smiled again when Tommy clapped his hands and ran up to the counter, trying to stand on his tip-toes to see over the edge. "I do believe I have just the thing. How about one of these giant muffins?"

Tommy nodded his head and rubbed his belly at the same time. "Can I have one, Mommy? Please?"

"You certainly can, Tommy." She turned to Mr. Willows. "We will be happy to have one muffin, please."

The mercantile owner let Tommy pick out his own muffin, then wrapped it for him. Before he handed it over, he leaned on the counter. "I think my beloved wife made me a special treat today. Would you like one of her nut butter cookies?"

Tommy slapped both hands on his cheeks and his eyes widened. "A cookie! Yes, please!"

Mr. Willows looked to Melody for permission. She nodded with a smile. It was so nice to have someone treat them normal, it was hard to believe the terrible treatment from yesterday ever happened.

She waited patiently while he wrapped Tommy's cookie, sliding an extra in for good measure. The bell above the door jingled with the arrival of two mature ladies. Melody hoped the store owner would hurry so she didn't have any more unpleasant conversations before leaving town.

"Annabel, I can't believe what I saw. Whoever those things belong to are going to be quite surprised to find everything strewn all over the side walks."

"You can't see two feet in front of you, Fern. Looters were helping themselves. I don't even know if there is anything left."

"I walked by about ten minutes ago and there were all kinds of clothing and dishes everywhere."

"Humph! Well, I walked by two minutes ago and it was all gone!"

"Two minutes? How did you catch up to me?"

"You're a slow poke, Annabel. I can walk ten blocks to your one."

"Oh, good morning, Mr. Welch." The one called Annabel nodded to the store owner. She squinted at Melody and then waved to Tommy with a shaking hand. "Hello, ma'am, little fellow."

Tommy waved back. "I've got a muffin for breakfast and two cookies!"

"Well, good for you," the older lady told him. "Now, if you are finished, I'd like to have Mr. Willows full attention. I've got a list a mile long today."

As Melody left the store, her heart lightened up. She had placed everyone in the same category as Thomas and the rest of the folks who were mean to her and judged without knowing the circumstances. She looked up to the clouds. "Sorry, God. I didn't mean to be so stubborn."

"Are you talking to God again?" Tommy stopped and looked up. "I wonder why he keeps hiding behind the white clouds? I want to see him."

Melody ruffled his hair. "Remember we talked about this before? I'll tell you another story when we get to PaPa Rusty's house. But for right now, you haul yourself up on the wagon so we can get our stuff and get out of here."

"When can I eat my muffin?"

She grinned. "You can eat it right now but save the cookies for later on. You may be hungry in another hour."

"Yes, Mommy." His little hands were busy unwrapping the cloth from the muffin. Melody was glad because when she came around the corner and pulled up in front of the hotel, she gasped. Pulling up her skirts, Melody got down from the wagon. "Stay here and eat, Tommy. I'll be right back."

Melody made her way to the cart where their belongings had been stacked. Hands flew to her waist as she recognized one of her hat boxes and a worn apron, lying open on the side walk next to the cart. Everything else was gone. She turned and marched to the front of the hotel as the manager came outside. He held up his hand. "You can't go in there," he told her.

It all came back now. The two ladies in the mercantile were talking about *her* things. Why had they been placed outside? "Sir, you told me my things were safe for twenty-four hours. How dare you put them outside for people to steal?"

"I assure you it was out of my control. I was ordered to move them." A red splotch brightened both his cheeks.

She saw Thomas through the door as he walked towards the entrance, a dark suit and a briefcase swinging in his right hand.

She tapped her foot, furious while waiting until he came outside. "Was this your idea of a joke?" Even though she tried to keep her voice down for Tommy's sake, it was apparent she was riled. Thomas almost looked guilty.

Almost.

She was learning he didn't have a decent bone in his body.

Another man hurried up to the two of them. Melody recognized him as one of Thomas's attorneys from their day in court. "Thomas," he greeted and nodded, unfolding a packet of papers before handing a paper to her.

"What is this?"

"Miss Rivers, as you know when you were married to Thomas, all your belongings became his. Upon the divorce, they also stayed his. Except for the urchin, everything you previously owned together belongs to Thomas. Read the paper you are holding in your hand and you will see it's all there, legal."

She glanced over the paper, unable to believe what was happening. "Did that give you the right to throw my things to the street?"

Thomas laughed. "They were no longer your things, but mine. Of course, I have no use for your belongings but there are so many less fortunate here in the city who do, so I ordered the hotel manager to place them outside to offer them for free."

She closed her eyes. If she dared to look at him, Melody was afraid she'd try to wring his neck! All her belongings gone in the blink of an eye! Tommy's clothing, his toys, all gone. She had one gown, and a shawl. A tear slipped down her cheek. She swiped at it, trying hard to be strong.

At least she had the horse and wagon.

"I hate you, Thomas. What you've done is wrong."

He shrugged, like he always did when not wanting to own up to his wrong doings. What had she ever seen in this man? He wasn't even a man. Disgust filled her heart and soul, a hatred of everything about him welling up inside.

Yet, she took a deep breath. All she wanted to do was get out of this awful city and far away from him. She turned to the wagon and Tommy.

Thomas grabbed her arm, his hand tightening around her wrist like a wrangler roping a calf. She tried to pull away. "Let go of me, Thomas, you have no right over me any more."

"That may be so, but you need to leave my horse and wagon here."

"Yours?" He wouldn't take her means of transportation out of here?

He nodded, squeezing tighter on her arm. "Mine. It's in the paper you are holding."

"It doesn't belong to you! Grandpa loaned me the horse and wagon while you were in law school so I wasn't stranded in Cooper's Ridge. It afforded me a way to go to the White Ranch."

"Mommy! Mommy!" Tommy climbed down from the wagon, running at high speed towards her. He had a horrified look on his face. His little hands were fisted in front of him. "Let go of my Mommy!"

Before she was able to stop him, Tommy latched onto Thomas's knees and bit his leg, hard.

Thomas yelped, releasing Melody's arm and stepped back, doubling over, clutching his thigh. When he stood upright, his arm lashed out. "Why, you little brat!"

He swung towards Tommy. Melody moved between them, scooping the boy in her arms before he got hit. Thomas's hand slapped her on the side of the face, almost knocking the breath from her.

Yet, she held onto her son, stumbling away, sucking air into her lungs. She wanted to turn around and hit him for what he had almost done but knew it was futile. He had the upper hand and she knew it. People began to stop on the street to watch the drama unfold. She had to get her and Tommy out of here before a policeman arrived.

Melody had fought too hard for the right to raise her son, he wasn't going to turn around and take her son yet, too. She took a final deep breath, raising her eyes to look him in the eye. "I'm getting my reticule from the wagon. You can have the wagon, take everything. Don't ever speak to me or my son again. My son, do you hear? You are dead to me!"

"I didn't try to hit you!" He flung out there as if that would make a difference.

She didn't bother to turn around. "No, you were trying to hit my son. Thank God my face got in your way."

With those words and her cheek stinging like the dickens, Melody marched to the wagon, grabbed her reticule from the seat and Tommy's cookies and walked away down the street towards the rail road station, hand in hand with Tommy using every ounce of dignity she could muster.

Digging through her reticule, she purchased two tickets to Wichita Falls, the closest town to the White Ranch. Since it would be another hour before the train arrived, they sat on the bench at the depot, her back straight, looking at no one except her sweet son whose life would be forever changed.

"May I eat one of my cookies?"

"Yes, of course." She patted his head, then hugged him close. "I love you, Tommy."

"I love you, too, Mommy. I love cookies, too."

His words made her crack a smile.

She may have a bruise on her cheek and her head a bit dizzy but it was worth the pain. No telling what would've happened if Thomas had laid a hand on Tommy. She'd probably be in the city jail right now.

No one was ever going to lay a hand on either one of them again.

Chapter 4

"I need to use the wagon for awhile!"

The desperation in Rusty's voice drew Adam's attention. The older man's cheeks were bright red, matching the color of his flattened hair. Rusty stood in the middle of Nora's kitchen, body tense, his breathing labored with hat in hand as if he had ran a mile to get here.

Adam hadn't gone to the barn to play cards with his brothers. He sat with his Ma at the kitchen table, finalizing the completion of the new cabin they just built. She had wanted to discuss the pattern for the curtains. Adam was rather bored and didn't care about any colors or patterns, but his Ma insisted he participate. If it made her happy, he'd sit here all evening.

"What's going on, Rusty?"

Nora stood when she saw how exasperated the man was. "Oh, Rusty, what is wrong? Why are you in an uproar?"

"It's my grand daughter and great grandson!"

Adam pushed his chair back to stand alongside his Ma. "Melody?"

Rusty raised a hand up. "Hold on, there. My hearts racing a mile a minute. All I know is our neighbor to the west was in town and came in with a note from Doc James." He opened his fist to show a piece of paper all crumbled up.

Nora moved forward to swipe it from his opened hand. "It says Melody and Tommy are in Wichita Falls. Please come right away."

"Let's go. You got the wagon hitched?" Adam didn't wait for Rusty to answer. "I'm sorry Ma, this can't wait!" He gave his Ma a kiss on the cheek, picked up his revolver from the side table at the door and hauled himself onto the wagon bench before Rusty could say one word.

Nora stood on the porch while they loaded up. "Be careful. I'll let your brothers know."

The two rode in silence for some time before Rusty let out a long sigh. His eyes glazed over when he finally looked at Adam. "I wouldn't be as worried but the note was from the doc. That's never good news."

Adam had a tendency to agree. His heart raced across his chest. A trickle of sweat slid down the side of his temple. Not knowing why the doc sent the note was killing him. Melody and Tommy were alone in Wichita Falls, hours away from her husband. Where was he? Why were they there instead of in Dallas?

Rusty tightened a fist and rung it in the air. "I swear to you if that no gooder has done something to my grand baby or the little feller so help me I'll kill him!"

Adam stretched his arm to calm the old man down. He gripped the old man's shoulder, patting him gently. It was important they get to Wichita Falls without incident. "We don't know anything has happened, Rusty. Maybe she was coming to visit and something happened on the way. Let's try to stay calm until we find out." If it weren't for Rusty, Adam would have saddled the fasted horse and be there by now.

"Well, I told her if she ever has any problems with him, she should go to Wichita Falls and send a note. So that's what we got. A note. Seems to me that's a practical enough answer to my worries."

Adam knew Rusty was right. He began to push the wagon harder. Even though they were almost there, it didn't hurt to go faster. Five more minutes and he'd see the woman he loved again.

"I never did like that dandy city lawyer. He thought he was too good for her. Dangling all those pretty things in front of her at first and then when he got in to that law firm he left her at home with the little one ninety-percent of the time to fend for herself alone. Ain't how a man's supposed to act."

"It's a different time than when you were first married." Even though he agreed with Rusty, Adam had to keep keep him calm.

"Hogwash! A man ain't no different than fifty years ago. It's how you treat a woman. Don't matter what time or century it is!"

"Now calm down, Rusty. Don't make me worry about you yet, too. Another few minutes and we'll be coming up on Wichita Falls."

"About time," he grumbled. Rusty took off his hat, shook it out, sluiced through his hair with an open hand and flopped the hat back on.

Adam's thoughts were going in the same direction as Rusty. Where was her husband? If he was in Wichita Falls there would be no need to call on the grandfather. So, why did they send for him?

Melody had been in his life since forever. Even though she was married, his heart wouldn't let him ignore any cries for help.

He clutched the reins tighter and gazed up at the cloudless sky.

Lord, let her be safe. Amen. I know you are the one to exact vengeance but someone has to keep her safe. If someone caused her harm, let me wring their neck! You know who I'm talking about. Amen.

Adam wasn't good at praying. He hadn't been a one on one praying man since he was younger but it sounded good and came from his heart. Plus, it was exactly how he felt.

The wagon pulled in front of Doc James offices in the middle of Wichita Falls. Most of the folks were on their way home from prospective jobs, hurrying up the boarded walk. Shops on the main street had their signs turned to closed. It was the time of day when everyone hustled to get home for supper.

Rusty moved fast for an old man. He was on the porch before Adam had a chance to tie the horse's reins. "Where is my grand daughter?"

Nurse Ellie stepped outside, her hand out to stop Rusty. "Sir, please, let's talk on the porch first."

A fear shot through Adam. He stood on the street, unable to move his boots. This wasn't good.

When Rusty began to argue, she placed an arm around him and forced him to sit on the bench, kneeling down in front of him. "Now, sir, please, get a hold of yourself. I want you to take three deep breaths. One. Two. Good. Three."

A fresh tear slid down Rusty's cheek. He left it there unashamed. "What happened to my grand daughter? Where is my great grand son?"

Nurse Ellie nodded. "Tommy is fine. He's at Miss Addie's boarding house having some supper. There is plenty of renters there to keep him occupied while his mother recovers."

Adam's feet finally began to move. He stepped onto the porch.

Nurse Ellie nodded to him. "You must be Adam."

He nodded. "Yes, how did you know?"

She smiled. "She's been asking for you."

He moved towards the door, but she put up a hand. "Adam. Not yet."

He turned to the nurse. "Why not. What happened?"

"Come sit down here on the bench."

"I'll stand."

"Very well." She turned to Rusty, placing an arm across his shoulder. "When Melody and Tommy arrived here earlier today, she was despondent."

Rusty interrupted. "What in the world does despondent mean?"

"It means hopeless, Rusty. Let the lady finish." Adam wanted the nurse to let him go in but he knew he had to stand here and listen to her speech first. He was afraid to see what happened to her and yet he wanted to burst right through the door. She was on the other side.

Nurse Ellie nodded to Adam. "Melody fell from the train depot platform. Luckily, the Sheriff was right there and able to bring her right in. She's got a bad concussion on her head with terrible headaches and needs to rest in a quiet place for a few days."

Rusty sighed. "She's alright then?"

When the nurse nodded, he stood up. "Well, then what are we doing out here yacking. I want to see my grand daughter!"

Nurse Ellie stood. "I was not going to let you go in there in your frame of mind. You needed to know how to approach her. If she doesn't stir much, do not get excited. She needs quiet. I'll only allow one person at a time see her. Five minutes tops. Then you need to let her get some rest."

"Okay, I'll be quiet. I promise." Rusty pushed open the door, lifting his hat off before entering. When the door closed, Adam turned to the nurse.

"You're not telling him everything, are you?"

She shook her head and sighed. "I'm afraid when the sheriff brought her here she was dehydrated. I don't think she has had anything to eat or drink in the past few days."

Adam was confused. Why wasn't she eating? "What about Tommy? Is he alright?"

She smiled. "Tommy is fine. He mentioned some disturbing things about his father."

"Oh? What did he say?"

"That he's a lyin' cheatin' no-gooder."

Adam closed his eyes. "Where's Miss Addie's boarding house?"

"Right across the street. You can't miss the small sign on the porch."

"This won't take long. I'm going to see Tommy, let him know we're here while Rusty is with Melody. You sure she is going to be okay?"

Nurse Ellie stood in front of him. "She will be fine as long as she gets rest and drinks plenty of fluid. I believe she got dizzy from not eating or drinking. She needs to keep up her strength."

"We will make sure she does, thanks for taking care of her."

"It's my job. Adam?"

He turned back, one boot on the ground. "Yes?"

"She also had a bruise on her cheek and temple in the shape of a hand print. It is one of the other reasons she needs to stay quiet. The doc wants to make sure she recovers from both incidents."

Adam was speechless. A growing anger filled him up so fast he was too horrified to say a word. He swallowed. Nodded. He began to walk away. Adam heard the door close behind him.

He walked down the street, past the boarding house. Past the church and the small café near the hotel. He began to walk faster, his strides now longer, his hands still fisted at his side. The pent up anger had to be dissolved before he exploded. The hand mark on her face had to be from her husband. There was no other explanation.

Had Tommy watched? Questions flew through his head like a bull taking the fence post head on. Knowing he had to get a grip and find out exactly what happened before Rusty went off the deep end when he found out turned him back towards the boarding house. Rusty loved his family more than life itself.

Adam needed answers. He also wanted to see Melody. Sweet Melody. A woman who had his heart all along. His knock was answered by Miss Addie herself. "Mr. White, I think there is a young man who will be happy to see you."

"Adam!" The little fellow came flying through the house until Miss Addie scolded him for running.

"We don't run in the house, young man." Her stern voice didn't stop him from flying into Adam's arms. He actually jumped from the threshold and wrapped his little arms around Adam's neck, clinging on like a branch on a tree.

"We are having supper, would you like to step inside and join us?"

Adam felt more than saw Tommy's whole body begin to shake. His face was stuffed tight into Adam's neck. Adam shook his head. "I think we'll sit on the porch for a bit if it's alright with you?"

"Certainly. I'll check on you both in a spell."

Adam sat on the swing sitting against the wall. Tommy still clung to him, finally letting the tears flow, leaving a wet spot on Adam's shirt. He didn't care. The boy had been so scared.

"It's going to be okay, Tommy. Your Mommy is recovering and will be fine in a day or two."

He sniffed and pulled his head from Adam's neck. Little sad eyes stared into Adam's own troubled ones. "Promise? Daddy hit her hard."

Adam tried to keep himself composed. The boy wasn't supposed to see such things. "I promise she will be fine. Your mommy just needs to rest. Why did he hit her, Tommy? Can you talk about this?"

Tommy swiped the back of his hand over his runny nose and sniffed. "I was a bad boy." He began to cry again, his little cheeks puffed up.

"That's no reason to hit someone, Tommy. Why were you bad?"

"I was eating my breakfast and when I looked up he was grabbing my Mommy's arm so I jumped off the wagon and ran as fast as I could." His little body shuddered and he bit his lip. His little fists went into the air.

Adam hated the fact the boy had to relive the incident but they all needed to know what had happened. "Then, the lyin' cheatin' no-gooder went like this," he raised a hand in the air, "and called me a little brat and almost hit me with his hand, but, Mommy, she stopped him!"

Son-of-a-gun! Melody threw herself in front of Tommy to protect her son.

Tommy bounced up and down on his lap. "When I grow up, I'm going to go back and do this." The boy raised his fist up and slapped at the air.

He didn't blame the boy. He wanted to go there right now and tear that man into a million tiny pieces.

Rusty closed the door to the doctor's office, searching up and down the street for the boarding house.

Tommy waved and yelled. "PaPa Rusty!"

The old man saw them and commenced to cross the street. When he approached, Rusty cried out. "My boy! There you are! Why don't we take a walk to the church? I was told by Nurse Ellie they are having a service tonight with some singing. Would you like that, boy?"

Tommy slid from Adam's lap and took Rusty's hand. "Hi, PaPa Rusty. Can I sing, too?"

The front door opened. Miss Addie sure had perfect timing, as if she was listening to every word. Yet, there was no way for her to hear through the thick wooden door. "Well, hello, Rusty! You're just in time to have some dinner. There's a seat at the table for all of you if you'd like to eat."

"Don't mind if I do." Rusty bent down to Tommy. "How about we have some supper and then go to the church after?"

Tommy jumped up and down. "I am hungry."

Rusty patted Adam on the shoulder. "She's sleeping but go see her."

Adam didn't have to be told twice.

"Mr. White, wouldn't you like to eat first?" Miss Addie's presence at the front door intimidated many, but Adam needed to see Melody more than eat.

"I'm sorry, ma'am but I have to make sure Melody is okay. The nurse is allowing us in for only five minutes."

"I understand. I have one room available for Rusty and Tommy to bunk in. I'm afraid we are filled to capacity. You are welcome to rest yourself on our settee."

Adam ran a hand through his hair. "I doubt I'll sleep. Thank you for the kind offer." When Adam turned away from the boarding house his heart began to pound. Melody was right across the street.

He had longed to see her again even though she had been married. He knew it wasn't right but what the heart wants made it difficult for him to stop aching for her.

Even if his Ma had ordered a mail order bride he would always want Melody.

How was he going to stand living his life with someone else when all he wanted to do was love and protect his best friend?

Even so, whatever he had to do to keep her safe, he would do. Adam was sure Ma would let her stay at the ranch, even help to protect her from her husband if necessary. The law may be one way in the city but out here in the country they had their own way of doing things until they didn't. The coward would never step a foot on White property if he knew what was good for him. He prayed to God above she wasn't foolish enough to take him back.

Even if he had to go to Dallas to show that lyin' cheatin' no-gooder he wasn't going to get away with hitting on a woman, he'd find a way to let the coward know what he did was not tolerated in this neck of the woods.

Adam took a deep breath as he opened the door to the doctor's office. Nurse Ellie was in the exam room, cleaning up.

"Hi."

Nurse Ellie turned. "Good evening, Adam . She's in the parlor. We set up a cot for her in front of the fireplace. It can get cool some nights and we don't want her taking a chill. You go on now. It's over there."

Adam followed her pointing finger. He nodded and left, standing at the door to the parlor, which was open a tiny crack. He stood there, looking in at her sleeping form, the fire crackling as it reflected shadows in the room.

He pushed open the door slightly, making his way to her bedside. There was a chair by the cot but he didn't sit there yet. Looking down as he stood over her, she looked like an angel.

Her beautiful hair was tied back, a long braid over her one shoulder. He reached for the locks then stepped back, afraid if he touched her he would disturb her sleep.

He didn't have the right to touch her, she belonged to someone else.

Anger so strong struck him like a lightening rod. A red hand print on her cheek darkened her features. The glow of the fire lit up her face enough for Adam to see it clear as daylight.

The realization of what she had gone through had forced him to sit down. Flexing his hands into fists, a vengeance burning somewhere deep inside his soul rose up. He wanted to leave this moment to find the one who did this to her. Now that he saw the evidence, it was worse than he imagined.

The coward will pay.

A soft moan had Adam leaning forward. Melody's eyes fluttered right before she opened them. "Whose there? Tommy, are you here?"

Adam sucked in a deep breath trying to compose his anger for her sake. "Tommy's fine. He's with Rusty at Miss Addie's boarding house."

Her eyelids fluttered closed. "I'm glad. Adam." His name was but a whisper on her lips. She tried to lift a hand towards him.

"You should stay still, go back to sleep. Everything is fine. I'm here now."

He took her hand in his, pressed his lips to her palm.

"My best friend."

"Always, Melody. Best friends forever, remember?"

A slow smile spread across her face, barely audible but Adam knew she was remembering the time they poked their fingers to draw blood, claiming it made them friends forever. A simple act as kids would hold them together always, even if she was married to someone else.

She took her finger and brushed it over his as if that alone would make it real again. "I missed you," she whispered before her lids drifted shut.

Adam sat there, staring at her as she slept for the longest time. He knew he had been there well over five minutes when Nurse Ellie came to check on her patient.

After spending several minutes making sure Melody was comfortable, the nurse turned to Adam. "You may stay. She seems to be more relaxed with you here. I'll go across the street and let the others know. It isn't proper to allow a man to stay here but everyone knows the two of you are like family. I'll be here to alleviate any gossip. The only reason I'm allowing you to stay is to help my patient. I only allow this in certain circumstances."

"Yes, ma'am." Joy filled him up. He hadn't wanted to leave her and now he didn't have to. He'd sit here all night if it helped her recovery.

The nurse left the room, leaving the door ajar. She spoke quietly to someone out in the hall before the front door closed softly. Adam settled back in the rickety wooden chair, his finger still entwined with hers.

Her trust in him eased his heavy heart. As his eyelids got heavier, Adam dreamed of earlier years with his best friend.

Chapter 5

Melody knew Adam was in the room even if his hand hadn't been holding hers. How could she not recognize these working hands, the tough callouses on the insides of his fingers? Last night as she dozed off she sensed his presence, calming her spirit. They had always been best friends. She remembered right before she fell back to sleep the urgency to touch him, to know he was truly there.

If only she had told him how she had felt years ago. Yet, it was impossible to do after what she knew. When she had overheard a private conversation between the three brothers that day so long ago, Melody had known she'd never have Adam as a husband. The three brothers vowed to never marry, to never allow another woman on the farm.

They held a secret close to their hearts, promising never to reveal it so Nora would never know.

They thought they were the only three who knew.

They were all so wrong.

She knew the secret.

That's why Melody had married someone else. She knew there would never be any chance for the two of them. They had been best friends, still were as far as she was concerned. Because she loved him so much and respected his wishes to never fall in love, she had forced herself to back away as they got older. It still puzzled her that Luke had gotten married after making the promise not to. Did Abigail know the secret?

Melody had promised herself she would never reveal what she had heard. She had tried hard to keep a distance, to never let him know how she felt about him.

Except for the one time he had kissed her under the tree by the creek. It had been a mistake and yet it had felt so right. After a lazy afternoon of swimming, the two were relaxing on the bank drying off. It was a warm Texas summer, a slight breeze rippling across the meadow.

Melody had lain on her back in the grass while the sun dried her clothes. She loved the times when Adam took her away after a run with the horses, how they always wound up splashing and laughing in the creek. That time had been so different.

She had peeked over at his profile. He was on his back, his own clothes pretty wet. He had reached for her hand and she let him take it, not thinking anything more of the simple gesture. She had just turned away to look up at the beauty of the sky, staring at the white, fluffy clouds. "This is perfect," she had said.

He had moved, turning on his side, his hand still holding hers. Adam rested on his elbow, and she felt his eyes on her. When he spoke the intent in his voice had startled yet excited her. "You're perfect," he had said, his voice, low, husky.

She turned, knowing full well he was going to kiss her.

Melody didn't try to stop him. She no longer cared about the private conversation she had heard earlier that week. She was curious how his lips would feel against hers. Even though she knew nothing would ever become of the two of them, she wanted this moment. For him. For her. For the two of them to take with them wherever they wound up. She remembered so clearly how the ache so deep in her belly had made her shiver.

He dipped his head at that very moment, moving even closer. His warm lips had stilled, pressing against her own as if asking permission to continue. She pressed hers against his mouth as an answer, reaching up to touch his hair.

Melody had heard a soft moan and to this day she didn't know if it had been her or Adam. They had spent a long time by the creek kissing, laughing and kissing some more until his crazy brothers showed up hooping and hollering, teasing Adam when they found them. She grinned, remembering how Samuel had started making kissing motions with his mouth, hugging himself and smacking his lips together.

That's when Adam thought his brother needed reprimanded and jumped on him, starting a wrestling match that had all three of the brothers rolling around the meadow like three bears in a Barnum and Bailey circus. Melody had laughed so much back then.

It seemed as if Adam had been at her side through every single part of her life. When her parents moved away to Montana a week after she married, Adam was there to see them off with her because her husband had been in the city working. She had sobbed into his chest as he held and hugged her, wiping tears and making her laugh afterwards.

When Rusty had gotten hurt on the ranch and they didn't think he would make it through the night, Adam travelled to Cooper's Ridge in the middle of the night so she was able to be by her grandpa's side. Every move he made had always been one of caring, of trust and respect.

Something she hadn't ever known with Thomas. Looking back, the only good from her marriage was Tommy. She wouldn't trade what she had gone through if it meant not having him. He was her life, her world. She was lucky, most women were not able to keep their children after a divorce. Most women were not granted a divorce.

Adam had been here since last night. As always, he stood by her side, forever friends.

Thomas had hated Adam, always trying to keep her from coming to the ranch. If Thomas had truly cared for her, he'd have been grateful for Adam's friendship. Instead, Thomas would come fetch her in the middle of one of her visits and cart her back home acting as if he wanted to be with her. After a few times, when Thomas left her to go back to the city the next day instead of spending time with her and Tommy, she had thought he was jealous and it made her feel good because he had never paid much attention to her. How wrong she had been!

It took her awhile to figure things out. Turns out it wasn't jealousy but a strange need to own her and not allow anyone else near. Because if anyone got too close, Thomas would be found out. She had been such a fool!

Regret at ignoring Adam and placing their friendship aside was uttermost on her mind. She needed to tell him how sorry she was.

Because he was so faithful.

Loyal.

Even now, Adam was here. By her side.

"My brother Luke would say, a penny for your thoughts?" His voice brought her back to the present.

She turned to him. "I have so much to say."

He brushed two fingers over her mouth. "Shush, don't try to say too much right now. Just heal, get better. I'm here for you, always."

"I know, Adam. You've always been my best friend. I'm sorry I've let our friendship go."

He pressed his mouth to her temple, the same spot that was blotchy and red. "I want to kill him," Adam said, his voice filled with retribution.

She closed her eyes, thinking for a moment she wanted Thomas dead, too. Yet, after all he had done to them, their family, she was a good Christian woman. Wishing him dead was not the right way to feel. "He'll get his own, Adam. You wait and see."

Adam gazed at her, his eyes filled with something she had never noticed before. It was deeper, bolder than anything she had experienced with him. "Tell me what happened?"

She closed her eyes, not wanting to relive these past few days. "Promise you will spare my grandpa? He's getting up there in age, I don't want him getting too upset."

"He already knows something bad happened and it's your husband's fault. He was the first one here. Rusty saw the hand print on your face, then Tommy told me what happened."

A tear fell knowing she let her son be exposed to such a scene. "I'm so sorry Tommy had to go through this. If I could change everything, I would."

Adam sat back, his hand holding hers, the warmth calming her heavy heart. "He's a strong boy. He'll get through. He said when he grows up he's going to go to Dallas and do the same to your husband."

"My former husband you mean."

Adam's hand tightened around her fingers. "What do you mean, Melody?"

"It means we got a divorce."

"Is that a fact?"

"Yes, I am no longer a married woman. I have officially been refuted by the good citizens of Dallas. I hadn't any idea it would be so awful to be known as a divorced woman. Almost every single person gave me a wide berth as if I had some awful, debilitating disease. Thomas made it horrible for me to stay."

"I don't know much about city life but those folks have no idea how fine of a lady you are."

Melody closed her eyes, a smile crossing her cheeks. "You always know the right things to say, don't you, Adam? I'm glad you are here. It's been an exhausting week."

"That's why as soon as you are able to travel, we will take you back to the ranch."

"I was hoping you'd say those very words."

He stood up, ready to lean down to place another kiss on her forehead when the door flew open in the entryway and a familiar voice called out.

"Hello? I'm looking for my son, Adam White."

"In here, Ma."

Melody and Adam grinned at each other. Nora White came sweeping in like a tornado over a Kansas prairie.

She swooped through the open door, Luke and Samuel by her side. "My goodness, Melody! I was so worried." She stopped abruptly when she caught sight of the retched hand print.

Melody saw the look between mother and son but Nora composed herself. She gathered Melody's hands in her own. "I'm glad you are fine. Now, we will speak with the doctor to see if you are able to be moved so you can come back to the ranch to recover. Hopefully, to stay. Where is Tommy?"

"He's with Rusty at the boarding house."

"Good. I'll go on over to speak with Miss Addie. I do have some other business to attend to with her." She looked from Melody to Adam, a worried look shadowing her face.

Twenty minutes later when Nora returned, Tommy was by her side, holding her hand. He had a smile on his face. "Nora says we can live at the ranch! I am getting my own horsey, too!"

Melody watched as Nora gave her a look as if silently asking her not to refuse. "Tommy is correct. I told him as long as the two of you will be living there, there is no sense in him not having a pony of his very own as long as you approve. Why, my boys are going to go to Dallas right now to buy him one."

"We are?"

"Yes, you are."

"All of us?" Samuel asked, confusion dripping from his gaze. He had been awfully quiet through all of this, Melody thought. She watched the youngest brother, surprised he hadn't tried to crack a joke.

Nora faced her boys. "Yes, all of you. It is my understanding the horse and wagon Rusty gave his daughter has been left behind. Perhaps an inquiry on that will be made while you are there?"

Adam spoke up. "We will inquire, Ma."

Nora didn't know yet Melody was a divorced woman. Would his mother feel the same way once she knew? Would she be shunned by the very woman who had acted more like a mother since hers had gone to Montana? There was no time like the present to find out. She wasn't going to hide it any more. Not after what she had been through. Melody decided if no one liked her because of her divorced status, she would have to find another way to survive. "Nora?"

The older woman hurried to her side. "Yes, dear?"

"You may not want me at the ranch once you know the truth. I am divorced and everything I had was left behind because the law says it belongs to him."

An eyebrow shot up. Nora patted Melody's hand. "The truth is right before me, my dear. The truth is, a horrible man, presumably your prior husband, has hurt you so bad you wound up on a cot half dead in a doctor's office. The truth is I don't care about any other truths. You are my family. Tommy is my family just as Rusty is. I won't tolerate this type of behavior and that is why my sons have to leave right now and get Tommy a horsey. He should have happiness surrounding him and he needs something to keep his mind busy." She turned to her boys. "I think Tommy needs a pony."

"Yes, ma'am." The three spoke at once.

Adam placed a quick kiss on Melody's forehead. Tommy's little arms went around Nora's skirt. "You are the best rancher woman in the whole world!"

Nora scooped the little boy up. "Well, I think we should go to the mercantile and fill a basket with some things you may need since you told me all your clothes and things were gone. Don't you worry, I brought a big wagon along for just this purpose!"

"Maybe Adam and Luke and Sam-you-el can bring back mommy's wagon and horsey, too! Daddy won't let us have them that's why we had to go on the choo-choo train."

Melody closed her eyes, ashamed Tommy's memories were of that time. She was glad to have Nora's help. As they all filed out, reassuring her they'd be back as soon as the doctor gave permission for her to travel, she settled back in the cot.

Adam picked up her hand, giving her a gentle squeeze. "I'll be back tomorrow with a pony for Tommy. If you happen to get released for travel, Ma and Rusty will get you home."

Home. All she was able to do was nod since she knew the tears were ready to flow. This family, the Whites, they cared about her. They were inviting her into their home as if she was a beloved member. Yes, it was where she wanted to be. Even if she was a scorned woman, they had treated her with respect. Tommy was being spoiled right now but he needed to feel he belonged.

And, so did she.

<> <>

Adam watched through the large front window of the mercantile while Tommy kept Nora busy showing her toys. Jumping up and down every time she nodded her head, he ran to the front of the store to plop another item on the counter.

When Nora looked up to see him through the window, she spoke to Tommy and came outside while the boy looked over some wooden trains. She breezed through the front door like she always did, her skirts flying around her. Nora knew how to make an entrance and an exit.

"We're heading to Dallas, Ma. Thanks for coming to take care of Melody and Tommy."

"Of course. Rusty and I will take care of things here. You make sure you get a healthy pony. Oh, and about that horse and wagon? Perhaps you may want to check on that while you are in Dallas."

Adam reassured her they had every intention of doing so. "Sure we will, Ma. See you when we get back."

Nora nodded before returning to the mercantile to help Tommy with his purchases. "Boys, be safe."

The three rode out of town, turning left towards the city. It was another few hours to Dallas which gave them plenty of time to plot the inevitable. Adam turned to his brothers. "We're not letting him get away with this."

Luke agreed. "You're right, Adam. There's no way. We've known Melody since she was young. She's like our sister."

Adam rubbed the whiskers on his chin he hadn't had a chance to shave. Tomorrow was Saturday so he'd get to it then. "We're going to have to be careful. The coward is a big city lawyer. He has the law on his side."

Samuel laughed. He clicked his horse to go faster. "If he can catch us. Ain't nobody ever done messed with the White boys and won."

Luke and Adam joined in. They tried to catch up to Samuel who was now in the lead until Adam got ahead of him. He looked back and grinned. No one wanted to up that fancy coward more than him!

It took almost two hours until they were in the city limits. When they led their horses into the livery, Adam spotted Melody's wagon tucked away in a corner of the yard inside a fenced in area.

The livery manager came out to greet them. "Howdy, names Welch. You men need to rest the horses?"

Adam slid from the saddle. "Sure do, may have to leave within a moment's notice."

Welch eyed the three with suspicion. "Why's that?"

"No reason, just wanted the horses ready to go in case we get called back to our ranch. We have a family friend who is ill and we're looking to buy a pony for her son."

Welch relaxed. "No, problem then. Forgive me, gentlemen, I thought you may be troublemakers."

"Nah, not us. We're here doing a favor for our Ma. Hey, by the way, you know who owns that wagon over yonder in the yard, the one in the corner behind the fence?"

Welch twisted around to see which wagon they spoke of. He nodded. "It belonged to a woman and her son. Came in here a few nights ago, scared to death of her husband. She claims he was a drunkard and she needed a place to hide out her and the boy. I let her stay inside the stable. She left the next morning but the wagon came back later that day. Some city lawyer owns it now. Makes you wonder what happened to her and the boy. I ain't never seen them again, but here's the wagon. Guess they sold it. Happens all the time."

Adam's hands were balled into fists as he stormed across the livery. "Any chance it belongs to a man named Thomas Cromwell?"

"Let me check my ledger. Why you so interested?"

Welch wasn't a stupid man. Adam had to be careful. Taking someone else's horse was a crime. But, before the night was over, he planned to have Melody's horse and wagon in his possession, one way or another. He shrugged. "Thought we may need a new wagon, looks like it may be affordable."

Adam turned just in time to see Samuel standing in front of a stall a few feet away.

Welch paged through his ledger. "Well, seems the owner is Thomas Cromwell. Lives in the hotel right down the street if you want to inquire about the wagon."

Adam nodded. "Much obliged. Do you have any ponies for sale? We're looking for one for our friend's five year old."

Welch knew every single horse in his stable. "Sure do. Where did you say you are from?"

"A ways from Wichita Falls."

Welch scratched his cheek. "I see, and you came all the way to Dallas to buy a pony when the Russet Horse Ranch is about a half hour from there?"

Adam looked at his two brothers, who were both trying hard to appear nonchalant. "Well, Mr. Welch, we had some business to take care of in the city so we thought we'd save us an extra trip."

The stable manager scratched his head and sighed. "I think I am putting two and two together."

"Yep, it adds up to four," Samuel piped up, looking for a laugh.

The older man didn't crack a smile. He was silent for some time until he nodded to himself and spoke up. "In the back stall is a pony I'm sure the little boy will love."

Adam turned to Welch. "I never said the child was a boy."

Welch grinned. "You didn't have to. I said I put two and two together. Now, gentleman, follow me. Let's take a good look at the pony. I'll even give you a good price."

The three men followed Welch, speaking softly so the older man wasn't able to hear. "Looks like we scored a pony," Luke told the other two.

"I believe so. Now all we need is Rusty's mare, the one in the first stall. He gave that horse to Melody when he bought her the wagon."

"You sure it's the one?"

"Yep, sure thing, Adam. She has a scar on her left leg from that time she ran into a nail sticking out from the barn," Samuel told them.

Welch spoke up then, interrupting their private conversation. "You know, if there's one thing I can't tolerate it's a man thinking he's better than someone else and beating on his wife. Why, just the other day there was a skirmish in front of that fancy hotel up the street."

"A skirmish?"

"Yep, sure was. Some man in a fancy suit slapped his wife, well, gossip has it they were divorced that same morning, so guess she was no longer his wife. Her brave son came to the rescue and bit the fancy man in the leg. Heard it took two stitches." Welch guffawed as he opened the door to the stall, bringing the pony out for them to inspect. "Talk went on all morning long how they had to leave on the train because no one would hire a divorced woman."

Adam made him an offer for the pony and inquired about the horse in the first stall, trying hard to keep calm. He hated the fact he was so close to that coward and had to keep from marching into the hotel and hurting him the same way he hurt Melody.

Welch scratched his cheek again. "Pony is sold to you, mister. No need to have your name. I'll take cash and as for the horse up yonder, I'm going to hook that one up to the wagon later on to make sure it would be a good fit. I'll probably have him and the wagon tied behind the stable. Maybe even tie the pony out for some fresh air later. And, I probably will be closed from six to seven for supper."

Adam, Samuel and Luke looked at each other. This was too easy. Adam handed over some bills. "Here's for the pony. I think she's worth more than what you suggested, appreciate your time." He threw a few extra bills to compensate for the profit the livery manager would lose on the horse and wagon.

"Thank you much." Welch mumbled to himself. "Just don't think a man should profit off someone else's misery he caused." He turned his back on the brothers. As they filed out, he looked up. "Oh, did you know that fancy lawyer at the hotel is having some big deal supper and award this evening? Be a shame if he were embarrassed in front of all his business associates. Oh, I don't know why I'm telling you this, you probably don't even know the man. Have a good day, gentlemen."

Welch retreated to the back of the livery leaving the three of them standing there in shock. Adam spoke up. "Well, men, looks like we have some work to do."

"Humph, I think I'd like to rent a room for the afternoon at that fancy hotel down the street. They say they have those fancy showers in there. What you say, brothers?" Samuel had a smile as big as a Texas Longhorn's horns.

Luke nudged Adam. "This is right down Samuel's alley. He is a joker."

Adam grinned. This night may turn out very interesting.

Chapter 6

"Thanks, I owe you one," Samuel told the bellhop. He turned to the other brothers, handing them a pin to place on their suit collar. "Are you ready for a great show?"

Adam nodded. He wanted to get back to Melody but the thought of humiliating Thomas in front of all his colleagues was too good to miss. Samuel had been working hard all afternoon to pull this off.

"Are we ready, gentlemen?" Samuel had a grin a mile wide.

"Let's hope this works," Luke told his youngest brother. "Adam, come on, stop poking around. The sooner we get this done, the faster we get back home."

The three men walked casually towards one of the private ballrooms where the law firm was having its annual prestigious award ceremony. There were partners and lawyers from several different large cities attending, making it easy for the three to fit in without someone realizing they didn't belong there. All three men were dressed in a three-piece suit, hair slicked back and a pin with the name of the Law Firm on their lapel to identify each person as a part of the ceremonies taking place this afternoon.

"You lucked out, Samuel. How much did you pay that bellboy to scarf up these pins?"

"Ten dollar tip. I told him we left our own behind and since we were new to the law firm we didn't want to embarrass ourselves by going in without one. See the small table in the back corner near the exit door? That's ours. I tipped another waiter to set it up for us, and if he asks, you have a severe case of anxiety and need to be near an exit in case you feel faint. In reality, I seated us here so we can leave early."

Adam wanted to march up to the front of the room where Thomas sat with a group of other men and drag him outside to give the same treatment Melody had gotten. He stopped himself when Luke took his arm.

"Calm, brother. This isn't the place or time."

Adam took a deep breath, following Luke. He sat with his back against the wall, turning his chair to stare at the profile of his enemy.

Ladies wearing identical uniformed dresses were scooting around the tables, clearing the many plates, dishes and silverware from the meal that had been served. The three men had been seated during the chaos so they wouldn't really be noticed.

"I got to give it to you, Samuel, you got us here so far. I can't wait to see the rest."

"Just get ready to go out through that exit door. Because when he realizes he's been hoodwinked, he's going to look for someone to blame."

A man stood in the center of the room, tapping a spoon to the side of a glass. "Attention, may I have everyone's attention, please!"

When the crowd shifted and got quiet, he began to speak about the law firm and how they would begin with the award ceremony. "My name is Daryl Hammond as most of you may know. I see we have some new faces here tonight. Welcome to all of you here this afternoon. I hope everyone has enjoyed the delicious meal. Coffee is being served as I speak. Let's begin, starting with the award for Thomas Cromwell." Daryl Hammond gave a brief lecture on the accomplishments of said person before asking him to stand.

"Here we go," Samuel said, nodding in the direction of a cute waitress holding a tray filled with hot coffee. She smiled and winked at Samuel then set a cup in front of Thomas.

"My, my, brother. You have an admirer."

Samuel laughed. "She is sweet but I hired her for this job. She's wrapping up a production at the theatre and was getting ready to leave on tonight's train. I met her at the clothing shop where I bought our suits this afternoon. After discovering she is an actress, I offered her a part in tonight's presentation and paid her and a few of her fellow actors to help out. Just wait and see what happens next."

The pretty waitress stopped by their table, whispering in Samuel's ear before exiting through the door.

Adam pressed his jaw tight as he watched Thomas lift the coffee cup to his mouth. Then Adam stared at the speaker, distracted by the words spewing out of his mouth, wondering if they were talking about the same person. "He is by far one of the most honest, capable, loyal and trustworthy persons I know. Please, give a round of applause for Thomas Cromwell."

Adam turned to look at the man he wanted to exact revenge upon when the whole room became silent. Several moments later, a bevy of snickers began as the crowd started to laugh, the eerie quiet turning to a flurry of hilarious guffaws and clapping of shoulders and backs.

Thomas Cromwell stood in front of all his colleagues in an expensive suit, smiling away while black ink covered his teeth and mouth. His face went from arrogant to puzzlement. He raised his hands out from his sides and shrugged his shoulders, drawing even more guffaws from the crowd then realized the laughs were on him. His look of fury on the man's face had Adam grinning.

Before the crowd was able to settle down, the double doors crashed open. Two women marched in, the one leading the way stomping through with a look of intention upon her face. She was dressed well-to-do, wearing an expensive gown with a thin shawl over her shoulders. The one behind her wore a hat with a wide brim hiding her facial features and a coat wrapped around her too warm for the type of weather in Texas. "Thomas Cromwell?" She spoke in a clear, loud voice that penetrated throughout the room.

Fingers pointed to the man standing at the table in the front of the room, his black mouth sticking out like a bright star on a moonless night. Adam leaned back, enjoying the show. What had Samuel done?

"Are you Thomas Cromwell?"

He nodded. "I am," he seethed, his voice barely audible.

"You, sir, are a disgrace! How dare you bed my daughter!"

"What! No! I don't know you, or her!"

"Mr. Cromwell, you have been sneaking around with my daughter, Prissy, for the last eight months. Now, look what you have done!"

She turned, pulling the other woman's coat away, revealing a full belly on the woman with the wide brimmed hat. A hand went to her forehead and she leaned back as if ready to swoon. "How dare you do this to her and then try to brush it off! I will not tolerate this. I have witnesses who saw you entering her window!"

Thomas shook his head furiously. "I am not the father! I hate kids! I don't know this woman, I swear!" He desperately looked around the room, his eyes flaying back and forth to his partners in disbelief.

Whispering began from one table to the next.

"What a show! You did good, Samuel. We better get out of here." Adam was ready to leave. If he wasn't able to do anything to Thomas, the thought of his humiliation tonight was going to live on for a long time. Even so, he wanted to get back to see how Melody was feeling.

"Shh, brother, we're not done yet!"

"I tell you now, in front of all of these fine people that you will not get away with this. Tomorrow morning, I have secured the priest at the Dallas Lutheran Church and you will marry my daughter!"

"That's brilliant," Luke slapped his brother on the back.

"Still not done," Samuel said, "here comes the finale."

Thomas stood with his arms hanging at his sides, trying to reason with his partners who looked horrified. He ignored the women, offering excuses the men weren't buying. "I swear, this is a joke. I do not know this woman and refuse to marry anyone!"

"That's a lie. You know me," the soft voice rang out. Everyone turned to the woman hiding under the wide brimmed hat, her soft spoken voice drawing everyone's attention. "We shared my bed, Thomas, or, Tommy-tom, as you liked me to call you when, well, I'll spare the details."

"I've never seen you in my life!" He began to walk towards her, fury in each step.

Adam stood. He wasn't going to let the man lift a hand to another woman, no matter if this was a theatrical spoof. Cromwell clearly didn't know the woman was an actress.

Before Thomas got too close she ripped the hat away. The whole room gasped.

Thomas stopped in his tracks. His eyes widened in horror.

Adam threw his head back and laughed.

The woman behind the wide brimmed hat had the ugliest looks on a woman he had ever seen. Her nose was so big it even had a hook on the end. Pastey, dull flat hair so short it was unbecoming to a woman covered barely below her ears. Her chin was just as pointy and when she smiled she was missing all of her top teeth. How had they pulled this off?

"That's hideous," he heard someone close by say.

"Poor man, he's stuck with that hag!"

"We better get out of here, it's five o'clock," Samuel warned. "Shows over."

The damage was done, now they needed to get to the horse and wagon before anyone saw them.

The three brothers slipped out the exit while the two women marched from the room, vowing if he didn't show up at the church in the morning the man would pay dearly! Adam knew the coward, he'd flee Dallas before facing another wedding. Hopefully, his life was ruined the same way.

"The ladies will be long gone by then," Samuel told his brothers. "Their train leaves at six. By the time Thomas figures it all out, his partners will have thrown him out the door like yesterday's bad news. Well deserving for the coward he is. As for us, let's get moving. We sure don't want to wind up behind bars." He stopped on the street, bowing to the other two.

"Come on, you are such a show off, we need to keep moving," Adam said, pulling Samuel by the arm.

Just as promised, the wagon and horse was tied in the rear of the stable, along with the pony for Tommy. It was going to be a long journey back since the pony would slow them down, but well worth the trip to see the coward get what he deserved. "We may be able to make it to Wichita Falls before sundown, men. If not, we'll camp out and head home at first light."

Adam was going to take every short cut possible until he made his way back to Melody. Hopefully, Ma had gotten her back to the ranch by now. He couldn't wait to see her.

This time he was going tell her how he truly felt.

<> <>

"Nora, are you sure you don't mind us staying here in this house with you?"

"Of course not! Why would you even think I would mind? To be honest, I love my sons, but I need more women here on the ranch. Thank the good Lord Luke smartened up and found himself a beautiful bride. Abigail is such a wonderful addition to our family."

"I agree. When will you let me help you? I've been sitting around here all morning resting. I'm tired of resting."

"Now, now, Melody. You heard the doctor's orders. He said another twenty-four hours and you will be out of the woods. I plan to make sure you follow the rules."

Melody smiled. "Thank you, Nora. You remind me of my mom at times like this. I miss my parents."

"You will have to send a telegram and ask them to come for a visit. I always enjoy your parents. Melody, do they know what happened?"

"No, they don't need to know, Nora. Not right now, they are enjoying their life in Montana. I'll tell them on their next visit."

Nora and Melody's mom had been friends for a long time, ever since she could remember. They had a special friendship where even though they were hundreds of miles apart whenever they saw each other they picked up right where they left off.

Melody felt the same way about Adam. The moment she realized he was at her bedside, her feelings went right to when they shared a kiss on the creek bank so long ago. It was as if the last five years never happened and she was back in his life where she belonged.

Abigail came through the screened door, a basket in her hand. "Good morning, ladies. Melody, so nice to have you here."

The two embraced. Abigail held her a bit longer. "I'm glad you came here," she told Melody. "It's for the best. City folks can be so cruel."

Nora raised a brow. "Abigail, I hadn't told you what happened yet. How do you know the city folks were mean to her?"

"Tommy let the cat out of the bag at my wedding reception. I've seen how city folk can be. I'm from Philadelphia, remember? I had a friend there who got divorced and had to leave the city in order not to be ridiculed."

Nora patted Abigail's hand. She smiled in understanding. "Thank you for being there for Melody. I'm glad she had someone to talk to since she is like a daughter to me. That's why I must speak to you both about Adam."

"Adam?"

Abigail poured the ladies coffee, handing each a cup. She sat down at the kitchen table across from Melody. Nora joined them at the head of the table.

"Yes, we must speak about Adam. Melody, I've hired Miss Addie to find brides for my boys. Abigail, being the first mail order bride knows how determined Luke was trying not to marry. Why, he almost sent her back. Seems there was a glitch in the contract I signed but thankfully he fell in love as I knew he would. Now, I have a wonderful daughter."

Melody wasn't sure where this was going. If she was ordering mail order brides for the brothers, that meant Adam was next. A small lump formed in her throat.

"Thank you, Nora. I feel loved here. You are a wonderful mother as well." Abigail wiped at her tears. It was apparently clear the two were close.

While the two ladies were paying each other compliments, Melody was preparing her mind for Nora's next words. She had a hunch about Nora's next words..

She just didn't want her to say it.

"Ladies, these past months we have been building Adam's new home not far from Luke and Abigail. There is so much land here, I'm surprised Adam wanted to build so close to his brother and yet I can understand why. All my boys share a common thread."

Abigail continued to pat Nora's hand. "I believe that common thread is you," she said lovingly.

"It's family, dear. We are all part of one big, happy family. Now, I know my boys. They didn't want me being alone and while I understand why, I had to move things along for them. I knew once Luke tied the knot the others would agree, also. You'd think there was some secret between them the way they acted about getting married. Or a pact, like children make when they are young."

Melody wanted to cover her ears. Instead, she smiled politely as Nora continued.

"Well, now that Luke has honored us by marrying Abigail, I've sent for a bride for Adam. She will be here in two weeks time. Ladies, it's a busy time at the ranch so I'm going to need your help with some curtains and décor."

Melody's heart fell to the ground. What if she stood up right now and declared her love for Adam? Would Nora send the bride back? Her hand went to her stomach, she felt a sudden ache coming on. It wasn't up to Nora, or her. The decision for a bride had already been made.

By Adam.

He had agreed to a mail order bride.

Nora turned to Melody. "I'm so happy to have you here, Melody. You are like the sister the three boys never had. Especially Adam, since the two of you are best friends."

A sadness deep inside had Melody wanting to escape the room. "If you'll excuse me, I am feeling poorly. I believe you are right, Nora, I need to get more rest."

The two ladies helped Melody up the stairs to the room she shared with Tommy. "Thank you," she told them.

"Get some rest. Hopefully, the men will be back today. I'm sure anxious to see Tommy's reaction to a pony."

After Abigail and Nora left, Melody pulled the covers over her. She closed her eyes, trying to force the tears back but they fell anyway.

She thought Adam truly cared for her but realized it was time to face the truth. He loved her like a sister. Nothing more. Why was she so naive when it came to men? Of course he would hold her hand through out the night, staying by her side. It was no different than when they were younger, wasn't it?

He looked at Tommy as a part of the family. Everyone did. At least she had that. A deep sigh rose up. Nora had ordered a bride with Adam's approval. He had built his bride a new home.

She would continue to be his best friend until his wife became that woman.

She didn't blame him one bit for moving on when she married five years ago. Even though there was something between the two of them, neither one ever had a chance to say how they felt.

Why did Melody assume he would want her now? He never even knew she was getting a divorce. She had never once given him any idea the marriage to Thomas wasn't working out. He had no reason to assume anything except she was happy. Melody sniffed and wiped her tears. He deserved to have a life with the woman he loved.

She would not stand in his way. Even though it seemed as if there was something between them, she'd treat him like a sister. Stand back out of the way so he was able to find the love and happiness of a good Christian woman.

Like his mother had promised for him.

Chapter 7

"Mommy! Mommy! I have my own pony!" Tommy stood at the side of the bed, jumping up and down.

Melody must have fallen asleep after her bout of tears earlier. Pushing the covers aside, she picked Tommy up, setting him on her lap. He snuggled in her arms for a well deserved hug.

Then he hopped off her lap and began to bounce up and down on the bed. "Tommy! Stop that this instant!"

He settled down, sticking his bottom lip out in a pout. "I'm just so happy. Want to see the pony? Come on, Mommy. I want to show you!"

Since the doctor had warned her to take it easy for the next twenty four hours, Nora must've let her sleep instead of waking her to help with supper. When she got downstairs, Abigail and Nora were just about done.

"How was your rest, dear?" Nora stopped what she was doing to give Melody a hug.

"I'm feeling so much better. Tommy wants me to see the pony so I'm going to the barn to have a look."

Nora stooped down to Tommy's level. "Young man, I'm placing your mother in your hands. It is your duty to make sure she doesn't get overly excited about this pony. The doctor has not cleared her yet so you must take good care of her, do you understand?"

By the time Nora had finished, Tommy's eyes had widened. His shoulders went back and he stood taller. "Yes, ma'am, I will watch out for my mommy!"

He grabbed Melody's hand. "Mommy, you must listen to me, I am in charge."

Melody looked back to see the ladies trying hard not to laugh at Tommy's serious tone of voice. Instead, she ruffled his hair. "Lead the way, Tommy."

The two made it safely to the barn, as Tommy took Nora's words to heart. The pony was already put away in a stall for the evening. "I helped to brush him and feed him. Adam says it's my job from now on and he'll teach me everything to know about a pony."

"Well, then, lets take a look at your new pony."

As she paid close attention, Melody felt his presence before she saw him. There was an urgency in the air the moment he entered the barn. When she turned around, Adam stood there, his face clean shaven, hair slightly damp.

She smiled. "Hello, Adam."

He marched right over, gathering Melody in his arms. "Hello, Melody. I'm glad you are home."

She was home. This ranch had always been a haven for her. With his arms around her now, the need to escape never entered her mind. Not like it had in Dallas. Thomas's arms never felt like this, a safe place.

She was afraid her feelings for Adam were still very much alive. It was much more than sisterly love or a feeling of being best friends. How was she going to be able to live here and watch him with a new bride?

When she stepped out of his arms, Melody heard Tommy's soft voice in the background, coaxing the pony to the stall door.

For right now, she had to keep Tommy the main focus. She had to help him forget the terrible ordeal of having a father who didn't want him. Here at the ranch, Tommy would thrive and grow among these sons of Nora White. They wouldn't turn their back on him or call him a brat.

There was no time for loving Adam White. Not even for a moment. She knew she was welcome here for as long as she needed to stay so she would be grateful and appreciate the time here. Perhaps she'd go to Montana to visit her parents, take Tommy on an extended visit. It was too soon to think about anything else but making sure Tommy was safe and well taken care of.

Adam took her hand as they walked to the stall while Tommy talked away, explaining for the second time how he was taking care of the pony.

Melody tried hard to listen, to smile when appropriate and say the right thing. Her hand in Adam's felt nice, it felt warm and the tenderness in his eyes when he looked at her melted her heart.

She pretended for the moment things would always be like this. Like the three of them were family. Like they belonged together. She let the sadness go for now because Melody knew there would be many, many days ahead she'd succumb to the bitterness and devastation of losing Adam to a mail order bride.

At first, she thought maybe they'd have a chance to be together, but not now. Not if he were already planning to marry someone else. She would never ruin his happiness.

The sound of the supper bell rang loud and clear. Tommy patted his pony, waving goodbye and promising he'd be back to tuck him in bed.

They walked the worn path to Nora's house, Tommy in the middle, one little hand holding onto Melodys and the other Adams. Melody laughed at something Tommy said and looked at Adam, whose eyes were on her. They stared into each others eyes for a slight moment. When Melody turned away, she caught Nora standing on the porch, her hand still on the bell watching them.

"Hi Ma," Adam said, swinging Tommy's arm while they walked.

"We're hungry!" Tommy shouted out, letting go of their hands and running toward the porch. "Guess what, Nora? I'm going to put my pony to bed after supper. Want to help tuck him in?"

Nora looked away to smile at Tommy but not before giving the two of them a pointed look. It made Melody realize when Tommy let go and ran to the porch, Adam had folded her hand in his. It happened so naturally, she hadn't even realized it happened.

Supper time at Nora's house was always fun and interesting. Everyone always stood at their chair until a prayer was said, then the men would dig in like they hadn't eaten in two weeks. After about two and a half minutes of chewing food, more like gulping it down, the men would only then talk about their day. Satisfied, they'd retire to the porch where Nora always brought out one of her delicious desserts.

Tonight, everyone seemed distracted and quiet. Melody noticed how the men wandered off after a slice of Nora's special chocolate cake, wanting to turn in early.

Adam stood. "Tommy, if you want to tuck in your pony, we better go now. Do you mind, Melody?"

"Not at all, I'll help Nora with the dishes."

Abigail began to get up from the bench outside. It was a dark night, the moon's rays a dull light in the background. Even the stars weren't shining. "I'll help for a bit," she told the ladies. "Adam, do you mind asking Luke if he would walk me home a little early?"

Nora turned to her daughter-in-law. "Are you ill? You seemed awful quiet tonight, too."

Melody stood quickly to help. She had been pining away over Adam that she hadn't noticed Abigail's distress. "Why don't you sit, Abigail. Let me and Nora do the clean up."

Nora agreed, insisting Abigail stay put. Adam hurried to the barn to get Luke. Before the two ladies even went inside, Luke was at his wife's side. He picked her up in his arms and carried her off to their cabin across the yard.

Nora snorted, holding the screen door for Melody to go first. "I wonder when they are going to make their announcement?"

"What announcement? Oh, my! You mean? Abigail is with child?"

Nora nodded. "Not much gets past me. She's been feeling under the weather this past week, unable to keep breakfast down."

Melody began to stack the plates on a pile. "How wonderful! Your first grandchild. Do you suppose Luke even knows?"

"The way he ran up here and carried her home, I think he suspects and is waiting for her to let the cat out of the bag so to speak."

Melody tied an apron over her dress, dipping her hands in the dish water. "I'm sure she will as soon as she is certain. I can ask Abigail if she'd like to go to town to see the doctor if you'd like?"

Nora shook her head. "We should stay out of it, I suppose, however hard that will be. As for you, Melody, I'm glad you are here. I see you and Adam have remained very close."

"I am glad he is still my best friend. I don't believe I treated him very well while I was married."

"Oh? How so?"

Melody shrugged one shoulder. "Adam was always there for me. I didn't tell him about my marriage concerns. Aren't best friends supposed to tell each other everything?"

Nora smiled. "I suppose so, and yet there are always things we don't wish to reveal at times. I remember how Robert always checked up on me. We shared so much together. He understood when I wanted time alone so he allowed me to ride off across the prairie with my hair let down. I often rode for hours at a time. I guess we were best friends. But, we loved each other the way a man and a woman did, too. And yet, towards the end, there was something Robert had kept from me. I'm not sure what it was or if I'll ever know. He's gone now so it's not important. But perhaps best friends don't always have to tell each other everything."

Melody was touched by the story Nora revealed. The saddest part was Melody knew about the secret he had been keeping from her. She vowed to never reveal it and no one would ever know. It was time to focus back on Adam.

"Adam looks at me as his best friend. We are best friends. Nora, am I not supposed to feel anything more for Adam? Because, I'm afraid I do."

Nora set down a cup she was drying and turned to Melody. "It is probably too soon after your marriage and divorce, Melody. There is a problem having strong feelings for Adam. Or, romantic feelings. You know I love you like a daughter. But, he built a cabin for his new bride that will be here in two weeks time. Adam is a man of moral and will honor his word to go through with the arrangement. I don't want you hurt any more than you have been."

Melody bit her lip. Hearing the truth from his Ma made her realize the enormity of the situation. Adam would never be hers. She realized it last night and today but tried to forget a bride was coming to marry him. "You're right, Nora. I don't know what I was thinking. I've always loved Adam. You have no idea how much I've cared about him."

Nora took Melody in her arms. "Then why didn't you tell him five years ago?"

She didn't dare tell Nora why she had backed away. The fact she knew about the pact her sons had made so Nora would never find out about the secret was a large burden to carry. "I, I didn't understand my feelings then. I heard him say he'd never marry and I believed him. Now look, he's getting married."

Nora held her at arms length, a puzzled look on her face. "Oh, Melody, not you, too! I know my sons are hiding something from me but now you?"

Melody's skin stood on end. She would never betray Adam. Taking a deep breath, she laughed. "Oh, Nora, don't be silly. Your boys are always hiding things they've done. I'll bet they have so many secrets you will never be able to keep up with them all."

Nora stood back, hands on her hips now, staring at Melody. About a minute later, after Melody held her breath while smiling, Nora shook her head. "You are probably right. I've been the head of this family for so long, I'm starting to dream things that are not there. I'm sorry, Melody."

She busied her hands pulling off her apron, keeping eyes downcast in case the older woman saw the truth. "It's fine. Don't worry too much, your sons love you so much. Now, why don't we sit on the porch for awhile."

Nora yawned. "It's been a long day for me. You go ahead. Just remember my words concerning Adam. I don't want you to get hurt. Some day a nice man will come along for you to fall in love with."

After Nora went to bed, Melody stood on the porch, hands gripping the railing tight as Nora's words repeated themselves in her head.

It wasn't fair. She married Thomas because of the brothers vow to never marry. All three brothers had promised that day to stay single and never leave their mother alone. Now, here they are, five years later, Luke married to a wonderful woman and Adam about to be married. The only one not married yet was Samuel. All because of the sins of a father. She guessed the secret would remain between the three men. And her.

Why wasn't Samuel married yet? Melody peeked around the corner, listening for Tommy in the barn but all she heard were muffled voices. A thought began to grow.

She hurried inside to knock on Nora's bedroom door. The door swung open. "Melody? Is there something wrong."

"Why isn't Samuel married yet?"

Nora opened wider, motioning her inside. "Well, I am forbidden from ordering more than one mail order bride at a time. Miss Addie's rules. She says because the brothers are so close they needed time to adjust to each other's marriages."

A smile crossed her face. "So you have not ordered a bride for Samuel yet?"

She shook her head. "No, not yet. One at a time, that is all Miss Addie will allow. Not until we are sure Adam's bride works out. The contract has a three month trial period. If either one decides not to continue with the marriage, it can be annulled as long as the marriage bed remains pure."

Melody clapped her hands. "That's wonderful!"

"Wonderful? How is it wonderful? Do you realize how long this is taking? I'd love to have all my boys married by next week if it were up to me."

Melody gave her a devilish look. "Nora, I have an idea."

<> <>

Adam ruffled Tommy's hair. "Come on, son. It's time to go to bed."

Tommy yawned. "I don't want to leave my pony out here all by himself. What if he gets lonely? Can I sleep here?"

"I'm afraid not, Tommy. Besides, there are other horses in here to keep him company. I tell you what. When you wake up, we'll come out after breakfast so you can check on him?"

Tommy gave his pony a hug and crawled over the top of the gate. "Promise?"

"Of course, I promise."

"My daddy never kept his. Are you sure you won't have something else to do?"

Adam swung Tommy up in his arms. "Son, I will never let you down. But you've been let down so much that I'm going to have to show you. So you go on up to bed and you'll see first thing in the morning I'll keep my word to you."

Tommy wrapped his arms around Adam's neck. "Thanks. I love you, Adam."

"I love you, too, kid. Now go on, get to bed."

Adam sat on the step listening to Tommy's muffled words before he went off to bed.

A few minutes later, the screen door opened and closed. He knew it was her.

Even before she sat down beside him, Adam felt her presence everywhere. It was always that way between the two of them.

No words were needed. Adam slid over, placing an arm around her shoulders. She fit against him like she always belonged there. Like it was her place.

The moon shone brightly this evening. It was round and looked so close to the earth, brightening the miles and miles of ranch land that belonged to the Whites.

Melody sighed.

He loved her sigh. Always had. It was one of those noises you look forward to hearing. It made him feel as if his touch made her happy.

He knew in two weeks a mail order bride would be walking down the garden path to marry him. Adam closed his eyes, brushing a small kiss across Melody's hair. If he was able to change things, he would.

At first he wanted to throw caution to the wind, declare his love and insist she follow him to the alter.

But his word was his bond. He made a promise to his Ma. To the bride who was going to be here in two weeks time.

"What's on your mind this evening, Adam?" Melody's soft voice interrupted his thoughts.

"I'm so happy you are here, Melody. I hope you know this."

"I do. You've been my best friend since forever. I want to apologize for not telling you how unhappy my marriage was."

He leaned over to place a kiss on her cheek. Her softness had him inhaling her sweet scent. "I wish it were different," he told her.

She stared at the moon's rays, beating down on the land. "Between us?"

He nodded. She felt it more than saw him shake his head. "I've always cared for you. More than you know. It would be an honor to take care of you, Melody. To love you more than a best friend would. But, I made a vow to Ma to marry the mail order bride coming in two weeks."

The sadness he felt now that it was out in the open was about to destroy him. If he were any other man, he'd say to hell with the mail order bride and marry Melody.

Yet, he was not that kind of man.

A promise was a promise. A vow, a vow.

"You can always change your mind. A man has a right to do so."

"No, I don't break a promise." He took her shoulders. "Why, Melody? I know you feel the same way towards me. It's always been this way between us. We'd make the perfect couple and yet you ran away with that city boy?"

"I didn't think you ever had any interest in marriage or I would have stayed. Trust me, I wanted to be your wife since forever."

Adam swore under his breath. "I'll be honest, the day you came here a married woman, I rode the ranch for three days, cursing myself that I never told you I loved you."

"You love me?" she whispered.

"I do, I always will." He took her hand and kissed the palm. "I only wish the promise I made to Ma had never happened but I am a man of my word. I hope we can still be best friends."

Melody stood. She shook her head. "I don't think we can be, Adam. Your new wife will become your best friend." She took his hand and gave it a tug. "Let's go inside. It's getting chilly."

Adam shook his head, backing away. "You go on, Melody. I have some things to do yet." He turned and walked away, not looking back. When he heard the screen door close, Adam kicked the dirt with his booted foot.

He turned around to see her douse the oil lamp, darkening the kitchen. It was a quiet night, no sounds from the barn. Everyone had a long, hard day, turning in early, not even a card game tonight. Adam stood for the longest time, realizing by promising his mother he'd marry a mail order bride he was giving up everything he had ever dreamed of.

Melody had been out of reach for five long years. Even though when she first married, it had hurt him deeply, he had been determined back then not to marry and bring anyone home to the ranch because of the secret. Perhaps it had been his fault she married someone else. Except, she hadn't known of their pact to never marry.

But when Ma was determined to marry them off, and Luke had fallen in love, their long ago pact became void. Even though they'd never give up the secret, Adam had wanted to share his life with someone and so he agreed with his Ma. He gave his word.

Then Melody came home, divorced.

How would he live here every single day with a woman he didn't love and have the one he'd die for so close?

How was he going to get through this?

Chapter 8

"I thought I was going to get married at the church in Wichita Falls? I don't understand these sudden changes."

Nora smiled. "We want to give you the best wedding ever, so it has been decided that you will get married here on the ranch. We'll send one of the boys to pick up your bride when it's time. I'll notify the Reverend in Wichita Falls of the change."

"It doesn't much matter to me. I don't want you making a fuss, Ma. Simple is fine." Simple, fast and get it over with is what Adam was thinking. He had no heart for a wedding.

"Oh, leave it to us," Nora told him, turning back to finish discussing the meal plans.

As he watched their excitement, he wished Ma and Melody were planning her own wedding. To him. It was an impossible thought because he had promised to marry someone else.

He did know one thing, Adam didn't want a big celebration. "I wish you'd keep it family only, not a whole lot of neighbors and such."

"Oh, don't be silly, Adam. Now, don't you fret. We will plan out everything and all you have to do is show up." Nora looked at Melody, her face filled with excitement. Melody seemed awfully happy herself.

He had been moping around here for the last week and a half and the woman he loved was happily helping to plan out his wedding ceremony.

Melody looked up with a wide smile on her face, her eyes bright. "I hope you don't mind but I thought I'd invite a few of my friends from Cooper's Ridge. Oh, and the pastor wants to officiate at the ceremony. We don't even have to have the reverend from Wichita Falls make the long trip here. Isn't that wonderful?"

Melody sat on the far end of the kitchen table, an expectant look on her face as if she wanted him to be as excited as she apparently was.

Adam stared back a moment, hurt that she was able to get over her feelings so fast.

His voice came out more gruff than planned. "I'm fine with whatever you want to do." Adam turned on his heels and left, slamming the screen door in his wake.

It infuriated him even more when he heard giggles coming from the kitchen. What in the world had gotten into his Ma and Melody? They acted as if the whole world revolved around a stupid wedding. For all he cared, maybe he wouldn't even show up.

Adam saddled up and rode across the prairie, needing to clear his head. He rode long and hard until stopping by their favorite watering hole.

Reclining on the grassy bank, his mind went back to the days when life was easier, before Pa died. He thought about how three brothers had rode together with Pa each and every day, working the ranch, turning it into what it was today.

Even after Pa was gone, the three of them had always shared everything. Getting through the days watching and helping Ma recover from losing a husband had been hard. Having been left to carry the load of work on the ranch had been tough before they hired men to help. Yet, the three of them always stuck together, they had made a life on this ranch, a good life despite the sadness of losing their Pa.

When Melody and her parents came by for a visit, she had been his retreat. Spending time with her, riding, carrying on with his brothers, they all had become so close. For some reason, Melody had clung to him more so than the others.

Adam ached for her to be by his side. Once he was married, there would no longer be days of riding together or fooling around in the creek, or even sitting here, remembering how fortunate they were.

The woman he loved would eventually find someone else and he'd be married to his own mail order bride. From the letters she had sent, his mail order bride seemed a nice person and her looks were suitable and yet, she would never be Melody.

If he were lucky, his new bride would find him hideous and demand to be sent back within three months. He may be a man of honor but what if he made sure there would be no marriage consummation? What if he showed his bride there was a better life out there without him? What if he fixed her up with someone else?

Would he be able to pull it off?

Adam hung his head.

He was a man of honor.

Unlike his Pa, who had fooled everyone.

Adam would be honorable and follow through with a marriage to a woman he'd never love.

He smirked, picking a blade of grass and throwing it at the water in defeat. It had been heaven for one glorious moment thinking he'd try to make life so miserable for his new bride she'd run back to wherever she came from so fast it'd make everyone's head spin.

He stood, staring at the blade of grass floating in the creek. No use daydreaming. It was time to get back to real life.

To a new life.

Without his Melody.

His two brothers rode up on him so fast he hardly had a chance to turn around, yet he knew it was them. They must've saw him head on out this way. They were all smiles until they saw the look on his face.

"Everything alright?" Luke was the first to speak.

Adam nodded.

"I was gonna pounce on you but by the look on your face, I best just stay right here," Samuel tried teasing.

"Yeah, not in the mood for wrestling."

The two nodded in understanding, slid from their horses in unison and threw an arm across Adam's shoulder.

The three stood there for some time, in silence, letting the day drift on like the blade of grass slowly making its way downstream.

Finally, Adam spoke up. "I'll be married in a few days."

Luke nodded. "You sure it's what you want, Adam? There's always time to change your mind."

Adam shook his head. "I made a promise, Luke. I have every intention to keep my word. You know how important my word is."

Samuel gripped his shoulder. "You made the promise before Melody came back divorced. We know you still love her. You always have."

"You're pretty smart for a little brother," Adam told him. "It still doesn't change anything. I am a man of honor and will keep my word."

"Whatever," Samuel mumbled. "I gotta get back, and since there won't be a wrestling match here, little Tommy wants to ride his pony. I promised him I'd help before supper." He rode off by himself, leaving Luke and him to stare at the creek.

Adam waited for his oldest brother to start a lecture. "What's going on Luke?"

Luke nodded. "You know, Adam, Tommy is a fine little boy. Seems a shame for him to grow up without a father. You could be that man."

"It's too late, Luke. I've made a promise. I won't go back on it."

"If you're so sure, then I guess I'll let you in on my good news. You're the first to know."

"What news?"

Luke grinned. "Abigail is expecting. We're going to announce it at supper tonight."

Adam slapped his brother on the back. "Congratulations, Luke. You deserve happiness."

Luke locked arms with Adam. "So do you."

<> <>

Melody was furiously trying to keep her eye on the end goal and stay far away from Adam in case she slipped and told him what they were planning. She was actually amazed at how quickly Nora had agreed to the idea.

Everyone stood around the table for the evening prayer. She lifted her head and peeked to find Adam watching her with a guarded look. His eyes, oh, those eyes were so stricken, so sad. It was almost unbearable to see him like this.

She stepped forward only to feel a hand on her arm. "No," Nora whispered softly, as if reading her mind.

Melody listened, lowering her eyes. It wasn't time yet. He wouldn't understand what they were doing. His loyalty and honor were at stake here and they were going to free him of this but it had to be done the right way.

Saturday was only two days away but it felt as if time had stopped moving.

Nora gave Melody a smile of encouragement. "Sit down and eat, dear," she said, following suit.

The crowd of men began to pass around the food, grunting and gobbling it the second it hit their plate. It was quite lively tonight. Everyone seemed in a fine mood. Rusty, her grandfather, kept winking at little Tommy, as if they had a secret together. Melody chuckled when Tommy winked back.

After everyone was well fed, Luke cleared his throat and stood. Abigail joined him at his side. "We have an announcement to make."

Melody grinned at Nora. She had been waiting for this.

"Abigail and I are proud to announce we are expecting a child."

The whole table stood. Congratulations were in order, while the men shook Luke's hand and gave Abigail a hug. Nora let a tear slip down her cheek. Dabbing at her tears, Luke took his Ma in his arms. "Thanks, Ma. For everything. For bringing Abigail here, it changed my life."

"I'm so proud of the man you've become," Nora told him. She looked at her other two. "Now it's time to get those two hitched."

Everyone laughed while Adam groaned. "It will be soon enough for me," he complained.

Samuel piped up. "I've decided I'm never getting married. I changed my mind."

Nora gave him a shocked look. "Samuel, we spoke of this the other day. Do you remember you told me you would follow in your brother's footsteps and settle down?"

"I decided it's too much work. Besides, I have everything here that I ever needed. Ain't gonna get hitched, Ma. Not now, not ever." Melody didn't miss the wink Samuel gave his Ma. She let out the breath she had been holding.

If Samuel had changed his mind about marrying a mail order bride, it would be too late for her and Adam. But he was playing along, as they had asked him to. He did such a good job, Melody thought he was serious about never marrying.

Earlier in the week, Nora and Melody explained everything to Samuel. When he realized he was able to help Adam be with his true love by offering to be the one to pick up the mail order bride in Wichita Falls, he didn't hesitate to say yes. He agreed to marry the bride, even though she was meant to be for Adam. He'd just explain to her what happened and they would start their own trial marriage. Why wait three more months when everyone knew Melody and Adam were meant to be together?

Nora told Melody she was sure the newest bride would accept anyone, she seemed particularly intent on marrying the moment her boots hit the streets of Wichita Falls. Her last letter had seemed a bit desperate. Even Miss Addie had mentioned so.

It gave the Whites an advantage.

Because while Samuel was in Wichita Falls meeting the newest mail order bride, Melody was going to be walking down the isle to become Adam's bride. He'd find out at the alter.

It was a perfect plan.

Nora and Melody had plotted for this all week.

Now all they had to do was execute it on Saturday afternoon.

Was it wrong?

She wasn't sure but it seemed right. Adam was too stubborn for his own good, even his own Ma recognized this. She agreed the moment Melody told her what she had wanted to do.

"I have an announcement to make," Tommy's little voice got louder as the crowd got silent.

Nora smiled. "Go on, then, Tommy,"

"You have to come outside and see what I can do."

Tommy ran out on the porch and down the steps, not waiting to see if anyone followed. He ran inside the barn while the others dispersed to the porch.

While Tommy rode his pony towards them, he tipped his hat at the crowd out front. "I want to introduce you to my new pony. His name is Joey. I'm going to show you my new trick I learned from PaPa Rusty."

Everyone watched as the pony trotted around in a circle, Tommy sitting so tall as he led the pony one way. Then he switched it up and turned the other way, winding through the yard. It was a big feat for Tommy.

Dust rose as a wagon came barrelling down the lane like a runaway horse and carriage, disrupting Tommy's show. The driver pulled up directly in front of the house while everyone looked on. Melody spotted her former husband sitting in the driver's seat while a man in uniform sat on the other side of the bench.

She stood, furious. "What are you doing here?"

"I'm claiming my property," Thomas told her. "Your so called friends here snuck into the livery and stole my wagon and horse. That's a crime."

"Poppycock! There is no proof my friends stole a thing. Now leave here, Thomas. You are not welcome."

The man in uniform stood up. "As an officer of the law, I am here to inspect all the wagons and horses to see if said wagon and horse are here as stolen property."

Melody tapped her foot. This was getting out of hand. "You, sir, do not have jurisdiction here. Did you happen to see the sign out front?"

"Yes, ma'am, I did. I'm sorry to bother you kind folks, but Mr. Cromwell has reason to believe his stolen property is here."

"Shut up!" Thomas growled at the officer, probably someone he hired to come along. "I demand to be shown every single wagon on this property. I've been here before, I know where everything is kept."

A clicking noise silenced everyone, causing the crowd to look towards the front door. The one holding the shotgun stood on the porch, an intimidating sight to see.

Melody smiled. Her future mother in law was not one to antagonize.

Thomas pulled back the collar of his shirt in a nervous gesture. "You can't threaten me with a gun," he shouted out, his voice crackling, uncertain.

"Mr. Cromwell, you have less than thirty seconds to get off my land. This isn't the city, your police officer has no authority here. If I see a trespasser, it's my right to shoot him dead."

"I see. You want to play that way. I'll be back. This is not finished." He picked up the reins, his hands shaking. Melody doubted he ever met someone quite like Nora before, someone who wasn't intimidated by his threats.

Adam, Luke and Samuel surrounded the wagon. They stood there, an intimidating threesome. Thomas sat down on the hard bench. Sweat trickled from his brow.

"You heard her. This is private land. If we catch you here again, you won't leave in one piece."

"Is that a threat?"

Adam took a step closer. "I don't make threats, Cromwell, get out of here. Now."

"Yeah, get out of here!" Tommy's little voice shouted out over top the commotion. Pony and rider raced towards the wagon. Tommy's face was bright red but when he realized the pony was moving too fast he panicked.

Melody began to run towards him. Adam looked at her then at the pony and swore. Luke, Samuel and Rusty ran towards Tommy. Joey was spooked, he ran straight towards the wagon.

"Pull back on the reins," Adam shouted.

It was no use, Tommy let them go, sliding off the pony. His little body landed with a hard thump while the wagon in question moved out of the way, heading away from the ranch while everyone else was occupied.

Melody cried out.

Adam got to him first. He scooped the boy up, carrying him up the steps into the house. Nora cradled the shotgun in her arms, opening the door for Melody to get through.

Tears flooded her eyes. If Tommy were hurt, she would kill Thomas with her bare hands. "He had no right to come here!"

Nora placed the shotgun in its cradle, then enveloped Melody in her arms. "He will be fine. You take a look. I'll get a cold rag and some water."

Melody stood beside Adam. They both worked diligently, checking all of Tommy's limbs to make sure nothing was broken. When he didn't cry out, she felt a sigh of relief.

"There's no bump on his head. I didn't feel anything," Adam told her.

"Hush now, son. It's going to be fine."

Tommy's whimpers tore at her heart. He asked in his little boy voice, "Is Joey hurt?"

Melody smiled through her tears. "I'm sure he's fine."

Adam ruffled his hair. "I'll go check, son. You stay here and let your mommy take care of you."

She looked up at the man she was deeply in love with. "Thank you, Adam."

"I'd do anything for you."

Melody almost told him the truth.

Almost.

Chapter 9

Adam tried to adjust his tie. He was a man much happier in a plain button down shirt and pants. Just like Sunday morning church services, he didn't like shaving either. Except for today, his wedding day, he'd do it out of respect.

That was who he was. Loyal to his family. Honest. Above board and honorable. He was a man who did what he said, no matter what. Why then, did he feel as if he were making a grave mistake?

It was supposed to be one of the best days of a man's life. He looked in the mirror above the small dresser. It didn't matter how he looked. If Adam were honest with himself, he wanted to get on his horse and ride the range so fast and go far away instead of walking down this path to the alter.

He didn't want to marry the mail order bride. There was only room in his heart for his best friend. This new bride would never replace the woman he truly loved. Even though he had tried these past few days, no matter what he did, he wasn't able to get her beautiful face out of his head.

The other night when Tommy fell off his horse, Melody had looked at him with her teary, beautiful eyes and he almost took her in his arms and proclaimed his true feelings. Before he turned and walked out to check on the pony, he realized as long as she was on this ranch there would never be a way to keep away from her.

It wasn't fair to the new bride.

Would Adam and his mail order bride have to leave the ranch in order for him to have any peace of mind? Would he be forced to leave the only place he had ever known in order to forget her sweet face?

Confused and heartbroken was not a way to start a new marriage. Was it fair to the mail order bride? She had mentioned in her letter that even after the three month trial, she wished to continue the marriage, even without knowing anything about him. He thought it was a strange request but didn't have time to dwell there.

Adam made his way to the front porch when his two brothers ran up beside him. Samuel jumped him from behind while Luke swung around and picked him up over his shoulder. The weight made them all collapse onto the porch and a wrestling match began.

Sooner than later, the three were sitting in a heap on the front lawn, laughing out of control.

"Boys! This type of behavior on your wedding day! Adam, I am sorely disappointed!" Nora White stood above the three, hands on her hips. She peered down at them.

"I'm sorry, Ma! They attacked me, I had no choice."

Luke and Samuel stood up, brushing off the dust from their new trousers.

"The wedding is in a little over four and a half hours. Samuel, you best be on your way to the train station. Wichita Falls is two hours away, an hour and a half if you hurry. This will give you plenty of time to pick up the bride the moment the train comes in."

Adam sighed, frustrated at his Ma's demand. "I don't know why you want Samuel to pick up the bride. I can do it. She is my responsibility."

Nora shook her head. "I told you Adam, there are last minute touches to the cabin I prefer you do. Samuel is not a carpenter as we all know. You want it to look nice for her, don't you?"

"Honestly, I care little about how the cabin looks." He didn't realize he said it out loud until his Ma cursed under her breath.

The three men stood at attention. When Ma did such a thing, they knew she was done arguing with them, no matter how old they were.

She was about ready to let them have it and they all knew it, mentally preparing for her lecture.

"Luke, Adam and Samuel! I am sorely disappointed in the three of you and the behavior bestowed upon me this morning. Now, Luke, you have a wife to tend to. She will be needing help bringing food to the tables. Adam, I'll meet you in your new cabin in exactly twenty minutes and Samuel, get on your way. I expect you will be bringing a bride home to the ranch in four hours time."

Samuel looked up at his Ma before walking towards the wagon. "I'm doing this for you, Ma. You know how I feel about getting married. Three months, that's it! Okay, Ma!"

Adam and Luke looked at each other. "What's he talking about?" Adam asked.

Luke shrugged. "You got me. Dang kid must've knocked his head hard when we all went down. Look at the back of him, he's got dust all over his backside!"

Adam grinned. "We can't let him go into town like that."

Luke turned away, heading towards his own cabin. "Sure we can. He deserves to walk around like that, the way he's always playing tricks on us."

Adam headed towards his own cabin which was almost ready for his mail order bride. There were a few items to hang that his Ma thought were appropriate. Then, he'd be getting married in about five hours flat.

He pulled at the tie he wore, wondering why he hadn't seen Melody or Tommy this morning. Usually, they were right there in the kitchen with everyone else. He supposed they had slept in today since there would be so much celebration later on this evening.

Adam wasn't even nervous to meet his new bride. As he placed two shelves on the wall, his hammer stopped in mid-air. He couldn't do this.

Wave after wave of true, hard feelings for Melody began to stampede his heart. His chest pounded, the air in his lungs tightened until he didn't think he was able to breath.

Adam dropped the hammer. He marched from the cabin to the barn, where Roger was grooming some of the horses. Adam ignored him, instead saddling his favorite mare, guiding her towards an open field. He didn't look back to see the others placing tables and benches around the yard or bringing in decorations for the reception. Adam wanted no part of this wedding. He needed to get as far away as fast as possible!

An hour and a half later, he stopped at their favorite creek. He led his horse to the edge of the water to drink. She was probably thirsty by now. Adam stood on the bank staring at the water as it cascaded across the murky rocks and stones. Not knowing how long he stood, his horse nuzzled his arm.

Even the sun seemed to be dreary today. The clouds were overcast as if the whole world mourned with him. Adam sat down, throwing off his shoes and dangled his feet in the water. Memories of the days long ago when Melody had swam in the water with him, splashing and laughing, the sound of her voice echoing through the fields and pastures.

He hung his head, closing his eyes, trying to force her from his mind. Trying to forget a woman he had been in love with since forever was pure suffrage.

Adam sat there alone on the creek bank for almost two hours, contemplating his life. The days of cavorting on the creek banks were over. Even though Melody was back, they'd never be able to do the things best friends did any longer.

It would not be fair to a wife. The thought of spending three months with her then asking for an annulment struck him as clever at first until he realized Luke had tried that and failed. Even though he was so darn honorable, would he be able to explain to his new bride he was in love with someone else. Maybe he would be able to pass her off on Samuel. So many thoughts struck him right then.

He went over every option again and again.

Except when Adam thought he had a solution, his father's face loomed in front of him. Adam had thought he was a loyal, honest man. Everyone did. If he tried to dupe this bride, he'd be just like his Pa.

There was no way he'd be able to live his life knowing he was no different if he sabotaged his own wedding.

Adam stood, slowly making his way to his horse. Once in the saddle, he said a silent goodbye to the creek where it had all began for him. "Goodbye, Melody. I'll love you forever. Forgive me."

He rode off then, not looking back. From here on in, he was going to ride every part of the ranch except for here. It was time to forget about these memories and this sanctuary.

He had a wedding to get to and it was an hour and a half until he got back. Adam pushed the horse forward even though he didn't care if he was late for his own wedding.

<> <>

Melody stood on the porch while Nora straightened the hem. She didn't see Adam anywhere. It was two minutes until the ceremony began.

Pastor Murphy, with bible in hand walked over to stand in front of the porch where they stood. He was a handsome middle aged man with a smile for Nora alone. If Melody hadn't been so upset looking for a sign of Adam, she'd be considering the two of them as a couple. Was he the reason Nora liked to go to Cooper's Ridge every Sunday for church? It was an interesting concept.

Melody hung onto the small bouquet of bluebells in her hand, along with a spray of baby's breath. The pretty blue and white matched her pale blue gown she wore. Nora stood in front of her to arrange the matching veil over her hair. She draped the long piece over her face and gave Melody a kiss on the cheek. "I'm so glad we did this. My son is stubborn, he'd never do this on his own. Adam will be so surprised."

"I hope he hasn't fled," Melody worried. "I don't see him anywhere. Roger was in the barn hours ago and said he had gone out on his horse. Has anyone seen him come back?"

Nora placed the veil back over her face. "I know my son. He will be here. You may as well walk with Pastor Murphy to the alter."

Melody nodded in agreement. She stopped halfway down the steps of the porch. "Have you seen Samuel? Shouldn't he be back here by now with the mail order bride?"

Nora had a worried look on her face. "I believe he may have gotten himself tied up. He promised me he'd be here to watch his brother get married. We were going to have Pastor Murphy marry Samuel and the mail order bride right after your ceremony."

"Oh, dear. I hope she didn't get upset and leave. That would be a terrible thing if she came all this way to simply turn back."

Nora nodded. "Go on now, wait at the alter. I think I see your future husband."

Melody took a quick look to see a horse and rider coming in fast and strong. She smiled in relief, anxious for him to hurry.

She followed Pastor Murphy to the alter, holding the flowers in her nervous hands. What if he got mad and refused to marry at all? She hadn't thought about that part. Desperate to get this part of the ceremony over with, she asked the pastor to begin his speech to the audience, who were sitting in chairs and benches on the lawn.

"Are you certain you don't want to wait another moment? Your groom is now dismounting from his horse."

"Yes, please, begin."

Rusty began to play the fiddle, a slow tune unlike what he usually played. The audience settled down, their voices coming to a murmur and then silence. She peeked over towards the men while Luke patted his brother on the back before he two began to walk to where the wedding was taking place.

When Adam stood beside her, she lowered her head to stare at the flowers while the pastor spoke of faith, honor and trust.

"Adam White, take her hand."

Adam reached out. The instant their hands touched, she knew he was fully aware this wasn't his mail order bride. They knew each other too well. He had taken her hand too many times in the past. His breath hitched. "Melody?"

Her name being whispered on his lips caused Melody to turn to him. "It is I," she whispered back, trying to keep the tears from spilling over.

His words came out in broken sentences. "I told you I can't marry you. What are you doing here?"

She almost laughed at his confusion. "Oh, my dear, you don't get it, do you? We've switched brides on you. Nora helped, she knows all about this. Samuel left for Wichita Falls to marry the mail order bride that was meant for you. He agreed so it left you to marry me. We all know how honorable you are so we had to do this behind your back."

Adam stared at the woman he loved before he turned to Pastor Murphy. Everyone sat on the edge of their seats waiting for Adam to say something. "Pastor, get on with the ceremony." Adam wrapped his arms around her and lifted the veil, laying a kiss on her so deep she almost swooned. The tears fell as everyone in the audience began to clap.

"Whoa! Mr. White, please settle yourself. I still have a ceremony to perform!"

Adam let her go but not before stealing another kiss. "I love you," he told her.

"I love you," she told him back.

"Adam! Melody! Can I please conduct a ceremony?"

Giggles from the onlookers caused even the pastor to grin. Within ten minutes the ritual was finished. "I now pronounce you husband and wife. Adam, you may once again kiss the bride. A little less passionate this time, please."

The audience roared with laughter. Nora and Abigail hugged Melody welcoming her to the family. Rusty and Tommy began to stomp their feet and the fiddle began to get louder, it's music fast and lively. The others didn't hesitate to join in while Adam and Melody separated themselves from the crowd.

He swung her around then pulled her close for another kiss. "I don't know how you pulled this off, Melody but I'm glad you didn't listen to me."

"It wasn't easy. The thought of never being with you again, of watching you with another woman made me realize I had to do something. I love you Adam White."

He gathered her hands in his, dipping to kiss each knuckle. "I love every part of you, Melody. I sat on our creek bank for hours trying to forget you. It didn't work. Nothing worked. I wanted to come back here and call off the wedding. It just about killed me to walk the short distance to the alter. It felt like a hundred miles instead of feet."

"I'm glad came back and didn't call off the wedding. Because, husband, look at what you have now, me!" She brushed a kiss across his cheek.

He held her in his arms, swaying a bit even though the fiddle music was a faster tune. "I only wish you would've told me how much you cared five years ago. It would've saved us both so many years of heartache."

"Well, then I wouldn't have Tommy and I wouldn't change that for the world. But, when I heard the three of you in the barn that day, I knew there was no hope for me."

Adam stopped. "What day? What did you hear?"

"I was in the stall when the three of you came in, thinking you were alone. Luke made you all promise never to talk about the secret to anyone. I heard how the three of you vowed to never marry. I thought at the time I'd never have a chance with you, so when Thomas came along, I married him."

Adam looked deep in her eyes. "I'm so sorry. I had no idea."

"No one did. I've kept it to myself all these years."

He gathered her closer. "If there is any way to make it up to you, tell me. I've wasted so many years."

"No, like I said, we have Tommy. He was worth every moment we didn't spend together."

"He is. I love you, Melody."

"I love you, Adam."

She gazed into his eyes. A deep sigh escaped. "I know the secret."

His eyes widened.

She smiled, placing a kiss on his mouth. "And I love you even more for doing what you are doing so Nora will never know. It is safe with me."

Adam gathered her close. His heart beat heavily next to hers.

"Mommy! Mommy!" Tommy ran towards them, stopping when he bumped into their legs.

Tommy looked up with a broad smile. Melody's heart exploded. He was so handsome in his dark pants and white shirt. He even had a small bow-tie attached to the collar. "What is it, Tommy?"

"Can I call Adam, Daddy?"

Melody gasped.

Adam bent down and hauled Tommy into his arms. "You sure can, son." Little arms went around his neck as more tears exploded down her cheeks. Today was full of surprises, especially the ones she hadn't planned.

Nora and Pastor Murphy walked over. Melody still thought they made a nice couple. "Well, we pulled it off. Son, I'm proud to have Melody as my daughter. It was the only way you would do this without putting up a fight." She kissed her son on the cheek.

"Thanks, Ma. You are probably right. I can be so stubborn at times."

She winked. "Not at times, most of the time. Let's celebrate." Nora peered down the road at a lone horse and rider. "I wonder who that is? I wish Samuel would return, he left with the wagon hours ago and still isn't back. He didn't want to miss your wedding."

"I thought he would be here to marry the mail order bride?" Melody was certain he would be back in time for his own ceremony. It was how they planned this day out.

Adam squinted and then laughed out loud. "It is Samuel. Who in the world does he have along?"

They all began to walk towards the incoming rider. When Luke saw where they were heading, him and Abigail joined in.

Samuel lifted his arm in the air to wave. "Hello! No need for a ceremony! I'm already a married man!" His voice, filled with excitement also slurred a bit as if he had a tad too much to drink.

Nora placed her hands on her hips. "Samuel Adams White, are you drunk?"

He stopped the horse, sliding off and holding out a hand for the passenger. At first, Melody thought it was another man until they took off the wide brimmed hat. A flurry of blonde hair fell halfway down her back. She turned in greeting. "Hello, a pleasure to meet you. I am Mrs. White."

Abigail and Melody looked on in shock.

Luke and Adam grinned from ear to ear.

Nora gasped. "You are wearing men's pants!"

The woman looked down as if she just now realized she was. "Oh, that, well, I can explain."

Adam bounced Tommy up and down. "No need. We have a wedding to celebrate." He hooked his arm in hers and turned away from the rest of the shocked family.

"Let's go home," Adam told her.

Tommy bounced in Adam's arms. "Can I sleep over at PaPa Rusty's tonight? He said we'd get up real early in the morning and shovel the stables. He said I have to learn if I want to keep my pony. Mommy, what does that mean?"

Melody shook her head. "Oh, son, you will find out. Come here and give your mommy a kiss goodnight. I see Rusty waving for you."

She watched as he bounced across the yard, turning back to wave every now and again. Melody felt Adam's arms surround her from behind. "What a wonderful life we have."

Adam pulled her even closer. "All I care about is making up for all those lost years."

Then he swooped in, picked her up and walked across the yard like a man on a mission. Not looking back or caring if anyone saw, he kicked open the door to their new cabin, carrying his bride over the threshold and slammed the door to their old life.

It was a new life indeed with the one person she had always loved.

<><><><>

Thank you for reading Adam and Melody's story. Next is Samuel's story. Can you imagine bringing a mail order bride home to meet your Ma and she is wearing britches? What kind of woman is the newest bride? Who is she? Why is she wearing men's clothes as if she is in disguise? When Samuel meets her at the train station, he almost turns and goes the other way. But when she tells him her story he decides to help her. He's always up for an interesting time.

Next book is called The Bride of Samuel in the 3rd book on the Sons of Nora White series.

NOW AVAILABLE!![1] (https://www.amazon.com/gp/

product/B07BH5KJJ8)

---

1. https://www.amazon.com/gp/product/B07BH5KJJ8

Don't miss out!

Visit the website below and you can sign up to receive emails whenever Cyndi Raye publishes a new book. There's no charge and no obligation.

https://books2read.com/r/B-A-PXQ-DYVFC

BOOKS2READ

Connecting independent readers to independent writers.

www.ingramcontent.com/pod-product-compliance
Lightning Source LLC
Chambersburg PA
CBHW022200150726
47992CB00002B/887